"Don't Go,"

Lemon called after Renata.

She stopped and said seriously, "I'm not available for an affair or marriage. Leave me be."

His mouth said, "I'm not—" But it wouldn't go on and finish what he was not.

She agreed, "Fine." Then she turned and walked away from him, not swinging her hips in slow undulations, but striding along with level purpose.

Her purpose was to leave him. To get away. Lemon looked down at Hunter, who was regarding Lemon as he would a hopeless oddity. Even the *dog* knew the man had acted like a real dud.

Dear Reader,

Welcome once again to Silhouette Desire! Enter into a world of powerful love and sensuous romance, a world where your most passionate fantasies come true.

September begins with a sexy, sassy MAN OF THE MONTH, *Family Feud* by Barbara Boswell, a writer you've clearly indicated is one of your favorites.

And just as exciting—if you loved Joan Johnston's fantastic HAWK'S WAY series, then don't miss CHILDREN OF HAWK'S WAY, beginning with *The Unforgiving Bride*.

The month is completed with stories from Lass Small, Karen Leabo, Beverly Barton and Carla Cassidy. *Next* month, look for a MAN OF THE MONTH by Annette Broadrick *and* the continuation of Joan Hohl's BIG, BAD WOLFE series.

So, relax, read, enjoy…and fall in love all over again with Silhouette Desire.

Sincerely yours,

Lucia Macro
Senior Editor

Please address questions and book requests to:
Silhouette Reader Service
U.S.: 3010 Walden Ave., P.O. Box 1325, Buffalo, NY 14269
Canadian: P.O. Box 609, Fort Erie, Ont. L2A 5X3

LASS SMALL
LEMON

SILHOUETTE *Desire*®

™ Published by Silhouette Books

America's Publisher of Contemporary Romance

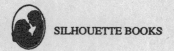 SILHOUETTE BOOKS

ISBN 0-373-05879-9

LEMON

This edition published by arrangement with Harlequin Enterprises B. V.

® and TM are trademarks of Harlequin Enterprises B. V., used under license. Trademarks indicated with ® are registered in the United States Patent and Trademark Office, the Canadian Trade Marks Office and in other countries.

Printed in U.S.A.

Books by Lass Small

*Lambert Series
+Fabulous Brown Brothers

LASS SMALL

finds living on this planet at this time a fascinating experience. People are amazing. She thinks that to be a teller of tales of people, places and things is absolutely marvelous.

One

Lemon Covington never did realize he was a mortal man. Born and bred TEXANS tend to be that way. That's because they've survived somehow, so they believe they're invincible.

Lemon stood six feet two inches tall. His hair was a light sun-bleached blond. His body hair was golden and made women's fingers restless.

Out in West TEXAS, where he was raised, it was a sparsely populated area. Resources were limited. No one guessed how handicapped Lemon was as a child, because he could fake about anything.

When he was finally tested, it had been a revelation to Lemon's parents to understand their only child wasn't the rebel they'd believed, he was dyslexic.

While all the other little kids in school had understood what was going on in class, there were those activities which had been a surprise to Lemon. He hadn't seen letters as the other kids did. He couldn't understand how the other kids could know what was supposed to happen when he didn't know.

He couldn't read and, frustrated, he'd rebelled. Since he was so hostile, the teachers in that tiny area thought he was simply stubborn and disruptive. A spoiled only child. His name was Lemon.

Was he really named Lemon because his parents took a sour view of him? Not likely. He was so named because the half lemon shell Don Juan was supposed to have touted as a prophylactic hadn't worked after all.

Eventually, Lemon's learning problem was diagnosed and he had help.

As an adult, Lemon was clean shaven, affable but shrewd. He never ordered anyone to do anything. He asked kindly. He was a thoughtful man who was gentle, and one who could talk anyone into doing just about anything. The fact he was aware he could, but didn't use the talent on guileless people, spoke well of him. He was truly a gentle man.

Lemon's dwelling was out in West TEXAS on the edge of forever. The place was aptly named Cactus Ridge. His big, old house sat like a clumsy ship riding the waves of mesquite. The usual ranch outbuildings barely surfaced in the lacy sea of the short trees.

The enormous house was from his momma.

His Trust fund was from his daddy.

At the advanced age of thirty-five, this only child was two inches taller than the neatly bearded John Brown, his financial adviser. While John was a quiet observer, Lemon was a participator, a talker.

The proliferating presence of Ohio Browns included Lemon as a friend. Besides John Brown, there were Susanne and Cray over in San Antonio, Tweed and

Connie over yonder at Sam Fuller's ranch, while Tom and Susan Lee were at the Petersons' and Mike and Sara were still at the army base in the middle of Texas.

That summer John Brown had been Lemon's financial adviser for around five years. Having been oblivious to an interested Margot for some time, John had finally really looked at her after she'd locked him in Lemon's library with her last New Year's Eve. There, she'd caught John's attention.

Cactus Ridge was out in the sticks and too far from other habitation. So it was easier for John to live in that great house. It was good for Lemon to have John there. John was raised in a kid-loaded house in Temple, Ohio. He well knew how to live with other people.

With all those Browns around that area in TEXAS, it was no surprise at all when Tom and Susan Lee came visiting at Cactus Ridge. The surprise was the big yellow dog that exited their car. John gave the dog a weighing look, but it was Lemon who exclaimed, "Tom, where did you get that scruffed-up beauty? I didn't know you had a dog like that."

John's visiting Margot came out of the house in time to hear Lemon's words, and she smiled at them all as she glanced at the dog.

Tipping his Stetson, Tom greeted Margot before he replied to Lemon. "I didn't know I had a dog, either. He was lost in the brush for some time. He'd been on his own for so long that he'd gotten edgy and careful. I left him water and food. Susan Lee and I were leaving food there when a wild boar bolted from the brush and chased me to the car. The dog saved my life. I got on top of the car, and Susan Lee was pumping bullets into the damned, unkillable boar the entire time, but she couldn't even slow him down."

Lemon slowly nodded in serious agreement through-out the retelling of such a hairy time.

Tom went on. "If Mr. Tiller, the postman, hadn't driven past just then and hit the boar as it crossed the road chasing the dog, I'm not sure what would have happened. But the dog had already saved my life."

Lemon said of the dog, "He's a fine animal."

Hunter went over to Lemon and just looked up at him for a while. The dog was so large that he didn't have to look up very far. He treated men as equals.

Lemon spoke to the dog, but didn't offer to touch him. The dog considered the man. Then he shifted his position to sit beside Lemon.

In a quiet voice, Tom exclaimed in soft tones, "Well, I'll be damned."

His brother John said, "Undoubtedly, but why now?"

With some regret, Tom explained, "Lemon, Hunter has chosen you."

Lemon asked, "For what?"

"He's going to stay with you."

"Now, why would he do that?"

"I don't know." Tom's voice was soft. "But you can see that he's aligned himself with you. I'm disap-pointed. I was getting used to him, but he's always been looking for whoever lost him. He's going to stay here. When we leave, he won't go."

Lemon chuffed in amused disbelief.

But when Tom and Susan Lee had finished their visit at Lemon's and were ready to leave, Hunter stood by Lemon and very slowly wagged his tail. Hunter watched Tom go to his car, but the dog didn't approach the car at all.

It was a tough time for Tom. He went to the dog and squatted down on his heels as he petted the dog and talked to him. Hunter licked Tom's face a swipe, but the dog didn't move away from Lemon.

It was a strange and touching occurrence.

Tom rose and said to Lemon, "See? You've got yourself a mighty fine animal, there. He's been around cattle. Geo says he's good with them. Take care of him."

Very sober, Lemon shook hands and assured Tom, "I will."

Tom got into his car beside Susan Lee and lifted a hand of farewell to the three people standing there. But then he looked at the dog with such regret. He started the car and turned it slowly, slowly, as if expecting the dog to run after him and bark for Tom to stop so that he could go along. But the dog did not move from Lemon's side.

As they drove away, Susan Lee said to Tom, "I would never believe Hunter could have brought himself to leave you."

Tom nodded sadly, "I thought he was mine."

"I'm glad you didn't insist."

And Tom smiled at his love. "He's as stubborn as you are. Are you still looking for the right man, too?"

She leaned over to put her head on his shoulder. "I've found him."

"Well, when a man has a woman and a dog, he can let the dog go if he can keep the woman."

She gasped as she laughed and swatted his shoulder. And Tom laughed.

Meanwhile, back at the ranch, Lemon said to John, "Want a good dog?"

John told his boss the obvious, "This dog isn't one you'll be able to give away. It was Hunter who decided on you."

Lemon mused, "I wonder who was the man who trained him. That must have been a wonderful partnership."

"Yeah." John was pensive.

Margot put in, "How did the dog get out there?"

"Sometimes it's good that animals can't talk. They're so opinionated, their talking could be a real nuisance. But at other times, it'd be a help if only for our curiosity."

The three stood there and the dog was equally quiet. Then Lemon said to John, "Help me shift that bunch to the other corral?"

"This isn't in my job description and—"

Margot burst in, "Let me!"

Lemon complained, "Good grief! Cattle and women don't mix. It's bad enough to deal with one or the other, but both at the same time is—!"

Margot retorted, "I can ride as well as—"

And John asked plaintively, "When does the crew get back?"

Lemon replied, "You're the guy who insisted they git time off."

John complained, "I get to nursemaid cows. Me. Do you know what Salty coughed up for me to get the schooling I had to have to keep track of you and your money?"

Lemon soothed insincerely, "Greenhorns pay good hard cash to do just this sort of thing?" That was a do-you-understand questioning statement. "Margot's willing. Why aren't you? Think of this as a perk."

Margot laughed.

John said darkly, "She shifted Adam's fig leaf first. That has to prove something about her mental evaluations."

"Well," soothed Lemon, "she's that type. And if you're lucky, she might just—"

"Careful." John's tone was a stern warning.

But Margot pushed, "Just might—what?"

John said, "You're too young."

"For what?"

"Almost anything," John assured her. "I'll lead you along slowly until you understand Life and Love and Responsibilities."

"That again."

Lemon demanded, "What...again?"

John told his boss, "None of your business. You're too young."

Lemon was indignant. "I'm a *year* older than you!"

John was superbly asinine in his kindness. "But emotionally you're untried."

"Oh, but I've tried. I've really tried. Even Margot turned me down."

John was indignant. "You tried for Margot?"

"When you were distracted by Lu—"

Margot instantly interrupted to correct him, enunciating precisely, "Her name is actually—Priscilla."

Lemon shook his head a little, licked his smile and said, "You're a terrible stickler. John, do you realize this hoyden is a stickler?"

"She'll come around."

Margot made an unladylike sound.

With all the other goings on, that was the day on which Hunter chose to stay at Cactus Ridge with Lemon. He was more help moving the beeves than

John, and John was no slouch. Margot was mostly an interested nuisance whom they tolerated. When the change was accomplished, she said, "It was a new experience."

The men sneaked a quickly exchanged brief, patient, rather droll glance.

Her family wouldn't yet allow Margot to move in with John, and their marriage was still a couple of months off. So Margot prepared to go home. As usual, John told her, "You're buckling down to the dictates of another era. Everybody lives together first."

She sassed, "Not my parents' children. Not even the boys!"

Since Salty and Felicia were exactly the same way, John really couldn't argue, but he did. "You're an adult. You can do as you want."

Margot asked, "Want to come home with me and try to share my bed? Daddy's bigger, and Sam and Phil are still home."

"You're nasty, do you realize that fact?" And she was flippant. He patted her bottom and told her she needed a firm man's hand.

But Margot asked, "Really? Where?"

And John looked up at the sky and groaned.

Margot drove off with an airy wave, leaving John starkly alone in that busy place. While it was only three in the afternoon, it seemed the sun was gone, and the summer earth was bare and lonely.

Lemon said in great good humor, "God save me from women."

John snorted.

Of course, Hunter had to meet the home pack. The leader was Dutch. Because Hunter wasn't interested in actually running the pack, Dutch was left alone. The pack stayed under Dutch.

It was July, and that summer's bridge tournament was at Cactus Ridge. Lemon's place had been selected by the committee because there weren't very many private places left that could handle that many people. Nor was there such house staff so readily available.

Cactus Ridge was so isolated that it was not a handy place to visit. Everyone came to stay, and it was a weekend of guests, meals and entertainment slid in between seriously played bridge rounds. Fortunately, the house staff was back from their holiday.

Being earnest players, Lemon and John knew almost all the guests. One was a real surprise. No, not Priscilla, who was known as Lucilla. She'd been expected. They all knew, by then, that Lucilla was earnest in her bid for Lemon, and that kind of bid had nothing to do with bridge. Lemon avoided her.

Then when Beatrice arrived, Lemon was coming down the grand stair in the entrance hall. He knew instantly that it should have been he who was coming in the door, and she who was walking down the stairs. Who was she? His self-protective shield came up. And the shield thickened when Lucilla came into the center hall from the library and greeted the new arrival with laughter and a cheek touching.

So the new unexpected arrival was of Lucilla's ilk? A witch who was clever, wonderful and deadly? Lemon had better be careful. So Lemon's face was only courteous instead of openly welcoming.

He said to Beatrice, "I'm your host. My name's—"

Her voice was marvelously soft and clear. She supplied his name for him. "Lemon Covington. How do you do?"

Lemon told her, "There's a map on the left wall of the upstairs hall showing where you'll—"

But Lucilla interrupted, "I'll show her, darling."

Lucilla had done that deliberately to mark him as hers.

Lemon gave Lucilla a cool glance and replied, "She can see it as easily as you did." Thereby, he implied Lucilla had had to find her own room in the same way that Beatrice would. He said to the new arrival, "It's up those stairs and to the left. All the rooms for the visitors are marked. May I wish you aces and kings?"

Beatrice smiled just a little, amused by him. "Thank you."

He added, "The gong meanings are at the bottom of the chart. Don't answer any unusual multiple soundings. Those are for the staff in case of trouble. For a fire we have an alarm. All that is on the board. I hope your stay is pleasant. Excuse me, ladies." And he left them there.

Lemon thought it was too bad Lucilla was such a brilliant player. Beatrice... Now why would he wonder about her? He wasn't going to play bridge. He had no desire to participate in a bridge marathon. He'd end up with Lucilla as his partner in the playoffs. She was something to avoid.

He was host because his house was so large. That was the only reason. That and his perfect house crew. While Lemon knew that he was being used, it didn't bother him. He liked company. But it was too bad he couldn't control the bridge committee.

He walked down the hall toward the library. Hearing Lucilla call to him, he turned into a side hall and disappeared.

The house was a kid's dream of a place. There were more halls and duck-intos and corners and closets with two exits. Whoever had built that house, how many years ago, had been quirky people.

Or they'd had untamed kids who couldn't stand the occasional bad weather, and the parents had *had* to escape somehow.

Lemon was going to make himself scarce. It was only for three days. He could handle that. He could always sleep in the barn.

Did this mean he was gun-shy? After all, he was now going on thirty-six. That was a little long in the tooth for a bachelor. Well, not necessarily. He was in pretty good shape.

With virile vigor, he strode along the back halls copying the new dog's confident movements. It had been interesting to see the dog's tolerance with the home pack. Hunter had been patient and only reasonably tolerant. He'd had to show Dutch he was equal.

Lemon went out one of the back doors and across the lane to the gate, through that and down toward the barn. He noted Hunter was alongside his own stride. How had the dog found him? He knew the place that fast? Interesting.

But what was he doing leaving his own house and going off? Whose house was it? Damn. Thank God John and Margot would be there to help. Lemon walked for a while, accompanied by the patient dog, and finally Lemon felt he could return to his own house.

He went up one of the stairways to his room and unlocked his door. When there was such a mob in his

house, Lemon locked his door. His father had suggested doing that long ago, and Lemon had found it was
a wise thing to do. Women weren't the only vulnerable
humans in this world. As his father had suggested, a
man didn't want any female surprising him. Lemon entered his room, allowing Hunter to come inside; then he
closed and locked the door.

The dog stood and looked around.

What did the dog see? It was a large room, the furnishings were treasured family heirlooms. Some clumsy
pieces had been handmade long ago and were revered.
One scarred piece was especially treasured. It had survived a Comanche raid.

There were pieces that had come from Europe with
ancestors. There was a solid German chest. And another was a small decorated Dutch one. The woods were
cared for, the trappings were elegant but subdued. His
room was like the rest of the house, which had been
"coordinated," but showed what pleased or was treasured.

It was with some great thoughtfulness that Lemon
should then consider that he was the last of his line. All
those families had narrowed down to him and his
cousin, Pots, who lived clear over in San Antonio.
Pots's name had been Potato Head as a child. That had
been shortened to Pots, which wasn't very flattering.
Pots had never seemed to mind being called so. His actual given name was Pottersby.

Pots was a tall man, well made, intelligent. He just
talked like a jackass. It was a testing facade. He was
good-looking and, at thirty-nine, he was surprisingly
still running around loose. That was because his Becky
had died in her first solo flight.

He was four years older than Lemon and as indifferent to being snared.

With the two seriously hunting women in Lemon's house, it seemed only fair that Pots should share the danger. He punched in his cousin's phone number.

"So?" That's how Pots always answered the phone. Not very interested, and if the caller had something to say, he or she was to get on with it.

"This is Lemon..." he began.

As was always the case, Pots then asked, "Anybody squeeze anything out of you lately?"

And Lemon gave the same old reply, "No."

"Your eyes must be bulging by now."

"No. I called to invite you to spend the weekend here at Cactus Ridge. There's a bridge tourney on. The committee decided to have it here. There'll be the bridge dummys who'll spread their cards and not care how their partners play them and they'll wander around. You can look them all over. The women, that is. Lucilla and several other tempting morsels will be in attendance, why not you?"

"She crowding you again." It was a stated question.

And Lemon asked in perfect sounding curiosity, "Who?"

"Lucilla." Pots was serious. "She dumped John to get at you."

"Bushwah. You do her a great injustice."

Pots asked seriously, "You trying to fool this poor, sly TEXAS boy?"

"Not likely. Come on over. Momma says I got to get you married off, if I'm to live in peace. You're the last of the line."

"So're you." Pots responded. "You getting m-m-m-m-married?" Pots always said it that way because he was allergic even to the word.

Lemon rejected such an idea, "No way, man. Nuh, uh! I'm living free and clear all by myself—most of the time."

"Then why are you picking on me?" Pots asked plaintively. "What'd I ever do to you?"

"Our parents are cousins?" Lemon needlessly reminded Pots. "They talk together, you're older, you got the nod. Get married and get some babies started."

"Why...that's a shocking thing to say to a young man like me, innocent and unknowing. How'm I supposed to do all that?"

Lemon was logical. "Get married."

"To *Lucilla?* She's been around the block too many times. She's probably incapable by now."

Lemon chided, "Don't be so fainthearted. Do your duty."

"Well, I'll come over to your place, directly, and look around. But I'm not promising nothing, no-how, no way."

Lemon assured him, "Your momma will be proud of the fact you tried. Get your bones over here. I have some of that sly whiskey you crave."

"Some of that gen-u-wine rotgut?"

"That's it." Lemon smiled at the phone.

"I'll come a-running."

"You do th—" But Pots had hung up.

With Pots there, Lemon should have more room, more freedom. Pots was a flirt. Nothing critical, but he was friendly. Lemon looked at his watch. He'd give Pots...exactly...one hour and thirty-five minutes. He'd land in the back on the dirt runway. Then he'd taxi the bug in far enough to walk to the house. Pots always did that. He hated jeeps and had a strong distaste for horses.

So Lemon decided to sell Pots the damned pinto horse that only Lucilla could control. Or...if Pots took to Lucilla, he could have the pinto for a wedding present! Yeah. He'd dangle the pinto for Pots.

Lemon went in search of Lucilla. And darned if he didn't have one hell of a time finding that woman. She was with Beatrice, and they were laughing. Lucilla saw Lemon first and she looked at him in a strange way. Beatrice became aware that Lucilla was distracted, and she turned and saw Lemon. Her look at Lemon was exactly the same as Lucilla's.

What did that remind him of? He'd seen that look.

But his steps had carried him to the women, and he returned their formal nods. He told Lucilla, "My cousin, Pots, is coming over."

Was Lucilla pleased? Did she respond in delight? No. She tilted her head back a little, and her eyelids closed down knowingly. Lucilla knew that Lemon had chickened out and called his cousin to come to his rescue. She did know. And so did Beatrice...probably. Beatrice had that same initial expression on her face. What was it?

Prairie wolves watching a sheep.

Lemon then excused himself to the ladies and mixed around in the crowd of potential bridge competitors, greeting old friends and nodding to acquaintances. The players were being sure who was seriously playing and who was there for the chance to meet with someone. It was a mixed bag.

With players who met at least three times a year, Lemon found he knew almost everyone. He'd hoped for somebody new and different and—of course—female.

He was again disappointed. He'd been attracted to Margot, who had eluded him even when John had been distracted by Lucilla for a couple of years.

By then, the one hour and thirty-five minutes he'd allotted Pots were up, and Lemon walked back to the rear of the house in time to see Pots coming around the side of the far fence... and he was with someone.

Someone shorter, and even more slender than Pots, was walking alongside Pots, and he was adjusting his steps to hers. Pots was never that considerate. Whom had he brought along? Lemon hoped to God she played bridge.

If she didn't play bridge, she'd play Pots, and Lemon would be left alone with Lucilla.

Lemon's mouth turned sour.

Two

Walking toward Lemon, Pots called, "Hello, Cuz!"

And Lemon replied kindly, "'Bout time you turned up. Even for a bad penny, you surely did take your own sweet time." While Lemon spoke to Pots, he was eyeing the woman in something like shock. Where had Pots found such a fragile dream?

Two of the interim hands followed Pots with the luggage. Lemon frowned at Pots, and as the two cousins met and shook hands, Lemon inquired, "Luggage? I thought you only traveled with a change of underwear and a razor."

Pots chided, "Now, you know our daddies cautioned us to always have a suitcase packed for emergencies. You calling me at the last minute, thataway, was a panic call. So, being the best cousin you have, I came."

"How long you staying?"

"I figured to chaperon you. You're vulnerable. You need back up. This here succulent bit is Renata Gunther?" That was a do-you-understand questioning statement. "While she is of legal age, her personality is as equally complicated as that there name of hers. I can't make heads nor tails of her, especially the—"

With easy patience, she spoke to Pots in an aside, "Cut it out." Then she offered her hand to Lemon as she said, "How do you do? I've heard tell of you."

Lemon looked into limpid, depthless dark eyes and became disoriented. But he was aware how very feminine she was. He asked, "Was it good or bad?"

She shrugged as if it was not at all important and commented in a dismissive manner, "A mixed batch."

While Pots har-de-harred over that, Lemon nodded slowly. He felt he was awash in a sea of turmoil. He frowned and looked at his cousin.

Pots had a bland expression that was rather smug.

Lemon looked again at the nymph. Although Pots had said she was legal, she couldn't yet be in her twenties. Her body was slender and very female. She was a little boggling for a "country boy." Then Lemon asked his cousin, "How come you came here?"

"You invited me."

Lemon frowned and his words were slow. "I don't recall expanding the invitation. This really isn't my party."

"I improvised." Pots's smile was patient and somewhat amused. "My room still vacant or did you let it out?"

"It's vacant." Then in spite of himself, Lemon turned his frown on the girl.

Pots suggested, "You got a bed for my friend? I would doubt you'd agree she could share mine?"

Lemon and Renata simultaneously made indignant sounds. She told Lemon, "He tends to act as if he's ninety and can say anything and be cute."

Lemon responded with strident vigor, "I've noticed that."

Pots laughed.

The hands had come up to them with the luggage, which Lemon took from them. "No need for you guys to lug that up to the house. Thanks."

Pots grinned and slouched as he waited for the exchange. Renata tenderly took her Vera Bradley suitcase of soft, gorgeous fabric. Pots allowed Lemon to carry his stuff.

"Where'd you get this leather one? I seem to recall it from other times."

Pots replied with the questioning statement, "It's my daddy's? You recall this family treasure?"

"Put it in a museum."

Pots complained to Renata, "He has no sentiment a-tall, a-tall. None."

So countering his complaint, she asked Pots, "You using your daddy's first car? I understand Ford still has parts made for those cherished antiques."

"Well, now," Pots slouched along, his empty hands in his pants pockets, looking around as men do, and he replied, "There's sentiment, and there's sentiment. My daddy's Model-T is in his garage, along with various and sundry other automobiles?" That was the do-you-understand questioning statement. "He has an alarm system and guards for those old, useless vehicles. Now this here suitcase still works, and nobody is gonna be stupid enough to steal something that cumbersome."

Lemon groused, "Think of the shoulders misaligned by this damned thing."

Pots chided, "There's a lady present. Watch your mouth."

And Renata added, "Yeah. Watch your damned mouth there, boy."

Lemon laughed.

Pots mentioned, "Where'd you get that deceptively scruffy-looking dog?" He pronounced it "dawg."

"That's an interesting story." So, as they walked along, Lemon told about how John Brown's brother Tom had found and fed the dog that had saved him from a wild boar. "They've inquired around. It's a good animal. But no one seems to know whose it was."

Pots said, "I'll ask around."

"Do it before I get attached to it. He chose to stay with me."

Pots nodded. "Being personally selected by a creature does tend to influence a man."

Lemon was sure. "It depends on what does the selecting."

And again Pots indulged his great amused laugh. Anyone within hearing distance would have to smile.

Inside the house, they had to move through the glad-handing greetings for Pots, who responded with chuffs of laughter and innuendos only understood by the recipient. And Renata was introduced in passing. The men were drawn to be introduced to her, and they urged to be allowed to carry her suitcase.

She again said it was a Vera Bradley and no one could touch it. She didn't mention that Lemon carried her larger one. He was host and immune to censure.

Upstairs, at the wall on the left, the three consulted the chart and located rooms for the two new arrivals. There were over fifty guests, and few had single rooms. Renata's small single room was across the hall from

Lemon's. He didn't mention that, but Pots growled, "You behave. Hear me?"

Lemon gave him a patient look. He had no inclination to dally with any female. The whole push of the intrusive weekend was to get through it unscathed by grabby women.

Lemon wondered if he would be as alluring to females if he didn't have all the things he'd inherited or been given by childless relatives? If he was alone in the world without any means at all, would he be that pursued? No. Without his acquired means and properties, he was just an ordinary man. Any woman after Lemon Covington was really after his possessions and position.

For Lemon, having Pots around eased the pressure. Pots was so gregarious and unassuming that no one ever realized he was in control. It was a talent.

Lemon's talent wasn't control, it was organization. He anticipated, smoothed the way and solved potential problems. He noted needs and filled them.

Pots manipulated people. Having surveyed the crowd of bridge players, Pots went to the phone and called a man to come along right away. Then he cheerfully insisted three more names be put on the board...knowing full well the games would be postponed long enough for his friend's arrival, while those in charge of pairing reorganized the partners.

That the postponement was accepted with only challenged interest instead of irritated annoyance, told how well versed Pots was in control. Nobody groused.

Lemon considered his cousin and wished for more of his genes.

Just before lunch, Renata came into the big reception room downstairs. She was in a flowing afternoon

dress in shades from tan to rust, which were so flattering to her coloring that the dress would cause any number of women to become hostile.

Through the standing crowd who was waiting for
lunch, Lemon went over to Renata and said kindly,
"This is going to be a weekend intensively concentrated on bridge, why don't you just go on home?"

She replied easily, dismissing him, "I'm going to
play."

He was taken aback. "You ... can?"

"Of course." In the crowd of talking, visiting people, she turned away from him, stretching up discreetly, looking at faces.

She was looking for somebody? She was watching
for ... Pots? He was right over there. He was the mag-
net of any room. Anyone in a crowded room knew instantly where Pots was holding court. She wasn't
looking for Pots. For whom did she search?

And Hunter came into the room, weaving around
among the people, causing some of the women to be
startled. He sure wasn't any sort of a lapdog. But
Hunter appeared to have sorted everyone else out, by
then, and he came straight to Renata. What a dumb
dog. She didn't fawn over him or talk baby talk to him
like others did. She laid a hand on his head and ignored him.

Lemon watched her hand and wanted it on his head.
Why? Why would that thought come into his mind? He
looked around for Lucilla and saw her laughing with
some other man. Good. But seeing that lure of a female trap strengthened Lemon's reserve.

He said "Good luck" to Renata, but he couldn't
quite leave her alone. And he found himself very reluc-

tant to introduce her to any of the people around him. Why was that?

He wanted her isolated and knowing only him.

He couldn't believe that. It was dumb. He eyed her with hostility and saw her as a charming, beautiful and quite young woman. He asked, "How old are you?"

"I wasn't aware men asked that of a stranger."

"It's my house. I need to know if you're of age."

"I am." She gave him a dismissive glance and turned aside enough for him to know with that particular glance, she had, indeed, dismissed him. She wasn't rude, but she was obvious. He was supposed to leave her.

He stood silently, trying to think of a way to walk away from her. He felt he needed to guard her. Guard her? There? He was losing it.

He frowned down at Hunter like he was in competition with the dog. Lemon wanted to be on his hands and knees in order for her to put her hand on *his* head? Surely not.

He stood, storm clouds roiling in his brain, not knowing why they were there or what they were supposed to do, and he frowned.

Lemon glanced around, and his glance was caught by Pots who was over yonder in a crowd, but his gaze was on his cousin, Lemon, and his eyes were very amused. Why? Lemon shifted and tried to appear indifferent.

People spoke to him, and sober faced, he nodded minimally, not encouraging anyone to pause. People did, and they talked to Renata. She introduced herself, since her host neglected to do that. Most of those around her were men.

Lemon reached through the crowding suits and took hold of her arm. She didn't come to him nicely, she resisted. His hand would not let go of her, and he was embarrassed by such a grip, but he pulled her toward him, saying "Excuse us," as if they were a separated pair and they were enroute someplace else.

He turned, ruthlessly polite, and led her into the main hall, which stretched clear across the house from the ballroom to the library. The bridge tables were set up in the ballroom.

She was silent. So was Lemon. Hunter trotted along. Since the dog was trotting, Lemon slowed enough so that Renata didn't have to half run to keep up.

She protested, "I didn't want to leave."

He replied, "I know."

She asked, "If you knew, then why did you insist?"

He was honest. "Damned if I know." And he gave her a silencing look as he pulled her along, with his hand on her arm in an iron lock.

She pried at his fingers and said, "I wanted to talk to my first partner. He had just introduced himself."

"He trumps aces."

"I've heard of his play, and he does nothing of the sort!"

He looked at her and asked, "How do I play?" And he was immediately appalled by his wordage because it revealed that was what he wanted.

She accepted the words at face value and replied, "Exceptionally well, but you're no shooting star."

He wasn't sure if that was good or bad.

She asked, "Where are we going?"

At least she wasn't screaming for help. "I want you to see our picture of Adam and Eve in the library."

"I've seen quite a few pictures of Adam and Eve. Naked people have seldom interested me."

"What ones did?"

"My niece. She is a love to draw."

"You draw nudes?"

"Of course."

"What sort?" he asked in a huff.

"Models. My niece—"

"Me?"

"No."

"Why not?" He was offended. "I have a good body."

"I don't draw naked men who aren't hired by the art school."

"You're still in *school?*" He was so shocked.

"I have a business degree. I'm taking art courses for my own pleasure. Artists have a rough time. Business is lucrative. Art rarely is. Money mostly comes after the artist is dead long enough not to get any royalties on sales." She then asked him in an adult manner, "Is any of this your business?"

He was still having to pull her along, and she was still resisting.

She asked, "Why are we leaving the others?"

"I don't know." But he was thinking that Margot had locked John in the library last New Year's Eve, and it had worked. Why not lock Renata in with him? Why did he even consider that? This was madness. Margot had known John for over two years. Lemon had only just met this stranger. He stopped and looked at her and thought madness wasn't all that bad.

She said, "Pots never mentioned you having any particular quirks. He considers you a stable, normal person. Not one who, for no reason at all, would drag a woman off down the hall, away from the other guests."

He nodded, listening, staring, and was aware that Hunter had followed. He now sat to one side. The dog was laughing with his mouth open and his tongue lolling out, he was so amused. Hunter thought Lemon was unstable. Not dangerous but amusing and controllable.

Lemon eased his fingers from her arm and released her gently.

She put her hand on her released arm. She moved her fingers subtly. She was massaging it to return the circulation? She thought he was unbalanced and should be avoided.

She said, "I believe I will go back to Pots."

He said earnestly, "I wouldn't harm you."

That surprised her. "I know."

He said, "You haven't seen Adam and Eve."

"I will another time. I need to see my first partner. We need to talk and exchange signals."

"Signals."

"For bridge. If I shift and cross my legs, he's to lead a heart."

"That's underhanded and wicked." He frowned at her.

She questioned, "Signaling?"

Seriously, he replied, "Crossing your legs for another man."

She tried to figure that out.

He was communicating with his errant tongue. It was a weird conversation. His brain was saying, For God's sake, she can cross her legs—under a table—as a bridge signal! And his silent tongue was replying heatedly, That's salacious!

Renata commented, "Pots said you are the most levelheaded man he's ever known. Makes you curious about all the others he knows, doesn't it?'' She turned and began to walk away.

"Don't go."

She stopped and said seriously, "I'm not available for an affair or a marriage. I'm not ready for either. Leave me be."

His mouth said, "I'm not—" But it wouldn't go on and finish what he was not.

She agreed, "Fine." She added rather pointedly, "Thank you for the hall tour." Then she turned and walked away from him, not swinging her hips in slow undulations, but striding along with level purpose.

Her purpose was to leave him. To get away. Lemon looked down at Hunter, who was regarding Lemon as he would a hopeless oddity. Even the dog knew the man had acted like a real dud.

He could join the Foreign Legion? Naw. He could survive the weekend and get past this fiasco. Why had he acted that way? It was totally out of character! He would have to be careful. He would take another look at Beatrice.

Why Beatrice, whom he'd just met and not Lucilla, who was very pantingly available? Lucilla frightened him. She did. She had panicked him into uncommon behavior with a nubile stranger. Naw. His clumsy approach to Renata had been all his very own personally sloppy and misguided try. How embarrassing for a man who was thirty-five years old to act as green and stupid as a thirteen-year-old throwback.

Lemon shook his head as he walked back and forth in the hall, making Hunter turn his head as the dog kept track of the strange man. He asked the dog, "Sorry you didn't go back with Tom?"

The damned dog opened his mouth, allowing his tongue to slide out as he panted with the humor of the man. Then he barked low and amused, one time. He understood the man exactly.

Thank God the dog couldn't talk and spread this fiasco around. What a juicy thing it would make on the gossip circuit. Smooth, old Lemon Covington acting like a ham-boned kid with a woman. He considered the dog. "Give me another chance. I'm really reasonably balanced."

Very gently, the dog scratched at one ear like the old pictures of Will Rogers. The difference was that Will hadn't used a hind leg. Other than that, the action was identical. The dog was amused and had no comment to make. There *was* no comment to make. It was all so basic that to comment would be insufferably redundant.

With mature stiffness, Lemon said, "I'm really quite grown-up."

The dog panted with his silent laughter.

Softly, Lemon inquired, "What's a barn dog doing in the house?"

The dog lay down, stretched out and rubbed his back on the precious Ottoman rug. He was privileged.

Lemon considered. "There's no way you could spread this as gossip. You can't blackmail me. Behave. Get off that rug."

Leisurely, the dog rolled over to his side and blinked lazily before he yawned. Then he got up and stretched before he got off the rug.

Lemon warned, "You're pushing it."

The dog happily wagged his tail.

"You talk to dogs?"

Lucilla came from a side hall. What was she doing down that hall? He considered her and asked, "Been exploring?"

"It's such a marvelous house."

His look was cold. He'd never forgiven her for her conduct to John. She'd used John.

Being charming, she suggested, "You should have a hide-and-seek party. There are so many good hiding places around. It would be fun."

She infuriated Lemon. He watched her with a deadly stillness, not replying and not encouraging her speech.

Actually, Lucilla hadn't done anything wrong. She was curious about the house and had investigated it. That was nosy, but it wasn't unknown. Once a woman had deliberately gotten lost in that house and three men had found her at separate times.

And Lucilla could ride his difficult pinto like no one else. She was alluring to males. Not to Lemon, but to most of the other men. It had taken John Brown two years to get past his bemused infatuation with this woman. She had discarded John. Now she was trying for Lemon.

She came to Lemon and put her hand on his chest. Lemon stiffened, and the dog gave a low, warning throat sound that was serious!

Both humans looked at the dog, who looked only at the woman.

As Lemon moved away from her lightly touching hand, he commented, "A male you can't lure? How incredible."

She wasn't stupid. She said lightly, "One of two."

"Well," Lemon said pleasantly, "no one can win everything."

"What does it take to win you?"

She shocked him enough. "I'm not a prize to be won." His reply was serious.

She knew that and smiled. "Don't wait too long before you choose."

"Is there a time limit?"

"The field closes." She shrugged her shoulders in a practiced manner that called attention to the movement of her breasts under the soft cloth of her afternoon dress. "The choices become too limited. I wasted almost two years on John."

Lemon tilted his head back to look down on her. "You never cared for John."

"I was fond of him."

"Not even that. You used him."

She considered Lemon. "Perhaps you are right. It was a grave mistake to have allowed him...the closeness."

"Actually, you were a good lesson to John, and to a good many other men who'd yearned for you."

"Did you?" she asked.

"No."

"I've wanted a taste of you."

"That sounds very sexy and alluring, but you're a cold woman."

"How can you know that?"

"Men talk."

That surprised her. "John!"

"No. Not John. To say that shows how selfish you are because after all that time you never really paid that much attention to him. He is very loyal to you, Priscilla."

Gently, she reminded Lemon, "I've taken the name of Lucilla."

"It's an elegant name. It's the name for an elegant woman. You aren't matching it. Why not act like an elegant woman?"

"Why are you so critical of me?"

"I believe it's because I care what happens to you."

"You're fond of me?" She smiled just a shade with excited attention.

"I admire your guts. Nobody else can ride the pinto the way you do. If you were a mare, he'd mount you."

"Ugh. That's all men think about."

"Yeh." Lemon bobbed his head slightly in little movements. "That about covers it. If you're that cold and revolted, why don't you get help so that you can enjoy sex?"

"Why don't you help me enjoy it?"

"I don't desire you."

"I've heard that men say all cats are gray after dark."

"That was Benjamin Franklin. There are men who are satisfied only to use women, but there are men who would love a woman who loved him."

"I could love you, Lemon."

So he lied. "I've lost everything in a rotten deal. Ask John. Go now and ask him. He'll tell you. I haven't the chance of a snowball in hell. This place and everything in it will go on the block."

Her shock was evident. She managed a very compassionate, "I'm so sorry."

Was her sorrow for him? Or for herself? He declined her compassion. "I have no responsibilities. I can survive. It's tough to lose this place. It's been in the family for almost three hundred years. If it all goes belly up, as a token, I'm keeping about ten acres near the creek's head. There's a cabin there. Want to come share it with me?"

She was stunned. She shook her head in tiny shivers. "You have enough problems without taking on the additonal one of a family. Is there any way I can help you? I have a necklace that would bring something."

"I'll give you the pinto."

"I don't want a horse." She dismissed his gift. "Thanks, anyway. I only rode him because it was such a lift to control him."

"Like men?" She had dismissed the gift. "Like controlling men?"

She smiled. "Probably. But with men, you don't have the reins. Lemon, you're a fine man. You'll make it all back. Is there any chance at all?"

"Not that I know. If anything can save any of my holdings, it'll be John. I don't know of another man as smart as John."

Her smile was a little bitter. "John." She said the name softly.

Lemon felt no qualms at all over being as ruthless as he'd just been. Feeling perfectly safe with her for the first time, he said, "Shall we rejoin the company?"

"I suppose. I am so shocked by your news. You're really brave to go ahead with this weekend, facing all that is to come."

"My parents would expect it of me."

"Is—their fortune involved?"

"I can only hope not. They have allowed me access to the grandparents' funds. That's gone. But my parents do still have their own holdings."

Lucilla made a sympathetic sound. It wasn't long before she excused herself and left Lemon and Hunter in the hall.

Lemon went over to a chair that was made of curved, polished longhorn cattle horns and upholstered with tail brushes covered with softened hide. The chair seat rested on the bases of horns with the points in holders on the floor. The arms were three sizes of stacked horns with the largest on top as the armrests. The tips held the chair back. It was marvelously made.

Lemon waited, knowing what would occur.

So it wasn't long before John came slouching along, his hands in his pockets, looking for the waiting Lemon. As John approached, Lemon began to smile. John said, "I hear you're going belly up."

"She proposed."

John took one hand from his trouser pockets, rubbed his bearded chin and walked a bit as he sought the exact wording. His words were mild. "You've ruined me as a financial adviser."

"Oh, but, John, you're going to save me at the very last minute."

"How about the grandparents' fund?"

"Even that! You are brilliant."

"She offered a necklace to help. I said it wouldn't be a drop in the bucket, and she should hold on to it." John stopped his careful, measuring pace and looked at Lemon. "It was a necklace I'd given her, and she's forgotten that."

Lemon groaned and said, "I hadn't known. I'm sorry."

"I'd always known she hadn't cared enough for me. Our relationship was different for us. I was ensnared, and now I'm totally free of her. There had been a slight, lingering nostalgia that has been banished."

"Good."

John advised, "The next time a woman tries to trap you, think of another way out. I will have a hell of a time comforting your friends and reassuring your businesspeople. This word will spread like wildfire."

"I told her not to tell." Lemon tried to bite his smile away, but his eyes danced with laughter.

"Your fortune's stability will be suspect for a while. You could have consulted with me before you threw us into this maelstrom. I could have thought of another, equally strong put-off for a voracious woman."

"Ah! That's what I told you about Lucilla a long time ago."

"I couldn't hear. My ears were blocked."

"How?" Lemon laughed.

"Not the way you're thinking."

Lemon told his friend seriously, "I am sorry for the inconvenience, John. You can handle it, I know that, but it terrified me when she suggested she wanted to be married to me, and I got out of it the only way I could— and as soon as possible."

John stood and looked fondly on Lemon, sitting in that marvelously grotesque chair. "How I wish I could have had your guts and knowledge. I suffered so terribly in my love for her."

"You weren't in love, you were bemused. She was a Lorelei luring you to be wrecked. And she damned near did it. If it hadn't been for Margot—"

"Yes."

Three

Pots's friend, Silas Miner, came that late afternoon. His plane landed on the dirt runway. He was rangy and at least forty-some-odd years old. His hair was as dark as his bushy brows and his hands were big. As he exited the plane, he groused about the facilities, "This track is damned cruddy, if you ask me." He put his Stetson on and hooked his thumbs in the pockets of his suit pants as he looked around.

Pots replied, "I'm glad to see you, too. I brought out the Jeep so's you wouldn't have to totter around on them there boot heels. You know how I hate Jeeps."

Silas's man efficiently took the luggage and put it in the Jeep, as Silas asked, "Where's a horse?"

"We've just got to smooth you out a little." Pots sighed over the improbability of doing that. He indicated the waiting Jeep.

Silas got into the vehicle and his man got into the back with the luggage. Pots drove.

Silas looked around, listening to Pots's directions, seeing the care given the land and the buildings; then they rounded the fence and saw the house. It was well done. Wood. Where had they managed to find all that fine wood to build a house that size? Money.

The two men exited the Jeep and went inside. Silas's man took care of the luggage. He would find Silas's room, make his acquaintance with the staff, the routine and settle in to be available.

Inside the house, Silas was still looking around. He noted the furnishings, the pictures, the ease of real elegance, which had never been roped off for display.

And they came to the gathering of people. Silas stood around, took off his hat and allowed his man to take it away. Silas nodded to this person or that one of those who were a part of the fascinating mixture of people.

He said to Pots, "Now what's the big emergency? Looks to me like this convention could yield up all sorts of problems. Who's the heart-stopper?"

Pots replied blandly, "She's frigid. She'll be grateful you already have kids. While she'll allow her body on occasion, she hates sex. But she has all the other requirements to run you and your establishment."

Silas smiled. "That kind."

"She would not only tolerate Margarita, she'd probably even allow her a room in your house and at your table."

"You jest." Silas's smile widened and his eyes sparkled.

Pots shook his head to deny that. "Nope. It is a real possibility. I need to tell you that Lucilla would undoubtedly convince Margarita to get schooling, and she'd probably take her shopping."

It had been a roll, up until then. Silas cautioned, "Uhhhhh."

"Your decision. I'm just presenting you with the option." Pots shifted his stance, put his fingers in the back of his belt under his jacket and looked benign.

Silas squinted. "There's a name for men like you."

"I'm more subtle, and I don't charge any fees."

Silas grumbled, then he shifted his feet to indicate a change of subject. In the TEXAS questioning statement, he said, "I understand they're having a bridge tournament? You get me in?"

"This is legit. No betting."

"Aw, hell. You're no fun a-tall."

Pots opened out his arms in a wide and vulnerable way. "It'll be a moral challenge." Pots coaxed in an arguing tone. "You can have fun without rigging the odds!"

Silas muttered a word that had gotten his mouth washed out with a soapy rag until he was fifteen and taller than his mother. He squinted over at the heart-stopper and said, "I'll have to take a closer look."

"You do that." As Lemon approached the talking pair, Pots said, "You're acquainted with your host, Lemon Covington?"

Lemon put out his hand and said, "I believe you're familiar with my parents."

"I tried to be familiar with your mother, but your daddy is a hard-nosed, selfish man."

"He is a tad possessive," Lemon agreed. "What did Momma do?"

"See this scar?"

Lemon smiled a little, "She didn't!"

"She sure as hell did. What a handful. I keep hoping your daddy sees the light and gets shed of her."

"No chance." Lemon patted Silas's shoulder. "Are you registered?"

"Pots did that. Who's my partner the first round?"

"Look on the board."

Renata came along, and Silas said, "Well, hel-lo!"

Lemon growled just for Silas, "No." Then he said to Renata, "A problem?"

"I find the partners have been shifted."

"Really?" Lemon was kindly interested.

"I got you."

"Why... how amazing!"

She said succinctly, "I understood the host wasn't to play."

"We've had some surprise guests who wanted to join us, and I was tapped. They needed another player. I was it." He smiled gently.

She eyed him and said, "Um-hmm."

Lemon moved her away from the two men, not introducing Silas at all, and he asked Renata with courtesy, "What sort of signals do you want me to know?"

She was a little stiff, and her lips were somewhat tight. "I don't give a partner signals. We play straight."

"But—" He began with earnestness, gesturing with a hand moving out from his body.

In a further distancing, she exclaimed, "I was trying to get away from you."

"Ohhh." He was so enlightened. His eyes showed a deer's innocence.

She felt like kicking him. Then, recalling what she'd been hearing, she said, "I'm sorry about your financial problems. Some of the people are getting up a purse to pay for this weekend. You are handling the disaster really very well. This would be an excellent time for you to return to school. You—''

"I'm dyslexic. School was a tough row to hoe."

She became interested and her whole attitude changed. "Was it colors?"

"How did you know that?"

"Some eyes need glasses of a color to read properly. Which is yours?"

"Red."

"Why aren't you wearing them if you're going to play?"

"I recognize the cards. I only wear them for craps." He wore them to hide his eyes when he gambled.

She put her little, comforting hand lightly on his arm and said earnestly, "If anyone can save your neck, John will."

"He's playing?"

She was kind. "He's your financial adviser, and my adviser says he's the best. You must have done something god-awful, and without John's permission, to've tilted your holdings this way."

"Lucilla tell you that?"

"No, it was Mary June. I am sorry. Especially for it to become known this weekend. Are you in the mood to just . . . play bridge?"

He smiled down at her and replied, "It's going to be okay. John Brown is a genius."

"To deal with an airhead like you— I am sorry. I should never have said that. You have enough to cope with besides listening to me."

"I like coping with you."

"Coping? There is nothing about me that demands that you . . . cope."

"If you cross your legs, do I lead a heart? A card or my own?"

"Good gravy. I can't believe you even asked. I have no signals...at all...about anything. Is that clear enough?"

Lemon bobbed his head a couple of times as if he was searching his brain for any traces of doubt.

With some impatience, she told him, "There is nothing more irritating than a man who pretends to be earnest."

That surprised him. "But...I am!"

"Bushwah." She stood straight and tried to hide her indignation.

He loved it.

With the three newly arrived plus Lemon, only another table needed to be added. So the delay was minimal. The tourney began, and Lemon was forced to play brilliantly because he wanted Renata to win. She was aware of his maneuvers on occasion and glanced at him with a pleased look that filled some of the cracks in his heart. When had he ever striven for approval? In all of his life, he'd wanted only to accomplish what he wanted. To read had been primary for so long. Just to read.

His mother had given up on him early on. He'd had manners drilled into him by his father. However, his dad was not only bigger but he was logical.

Logic is—logical. Such truths were also. Lemon could understand obeying or using logic.

But when he could go on as the one in control, all of his strivings were to satisfy himself.

Hiring John Brown had been a logical thing to do. That he also liked John had nothing to do with hiring him. If John had been a complete ass, Lemon probably still would have hired him. That was how competent John was.

Lemon had run his own life his own way for so long, that it was a surprise—on that day—to adjust his actions to please another human being. Renata. A woman. Why her?

Why her instead of a very willing Lucilla? How much time would he have had to spend with Lucilla? Even entertaining, they'd sit at opposite ends of the table. He'd never have had to exchange any weighty or lighthearted comments. They'd have had separate rooms, separate mealtimes, rare contact. She would have had her own bank account and her own cars, and they would have been separate people.

And Lemon finally understood exactly why powerful men married unsuitable companions instead of someone they loved, who would distract them from business. For the first time, he understood Pots inviting Silas to meet Lucilla. She would be perfect for Silas. A great hostess. She knew everyone, and she knew all the rules.

Lemon was dummy and put the cards down carefully so that Renata could select them easily. But Lemon didn't leave the table to walk around, nor did he go over to sit beside her and watch her own hand and the way she played it. No. He sat back in his chair with his arms folded across his chest and simply watched her face.

The flickerings of her decisions charmed Lemon. The pause to see which card was played by which opponent and the barest hint in the movement of her mouth or the flick of her eyes when she'd guessed right.

She was totally caught up in the game. She chewed her lip and pushed her hair around. She wiggled in her chair and she about drove his body crazy.

It was then he knew he should pass on this attraction. It could be fatal for his business expansion because she would come first. He would choose being with her and talking to her and teasing her and making love to her— Yes. She would come first, and his business would deteriorate.

Maybe not. John would handle that.

But John loved Margot. He would be distracted? Perhaps. Lemon continued to watch Renata play brilliantly. Would she be interested in the distraction of loving a man? She was intently concentrated on the Game. Bridge. Bridge could produce devotees just like anything else.

The real pros didn't snack or chat but simply played. And they remembered the cards for each hand with every play. Bridge could be addictive.

So could polo. Woodworking. Business. If Renata allowed Lemon close to her, could he become addicted . . . to her? It would be interesting to see.

What if he never got out of bed? What if he never let her out of his bed? Their meals would be delivered to his room. His phone would be beside his bed. He would have her always at his fingertips.

Lemon narrowed his eyes and considered why it was she who had boggled his thinking so easily this day. What was so different about her? He'd never before felt such a wild response toward any female. He needed to protect himself.

He'd heard tell of men who'd become some woman's slave. Look at John with Lucilla. That had been really a rough time for John. Even though she'd allowed him to stay with her, it had been on her terms.

When Lemon had finally told Lucilla to let John go, that Margot loved John and would be a good wife to him, Lucilla had been reluctant.

Lemon had had to offer a cash incentive. Then he'd had to up it as Lucilla said that John was such a convenience. In Lucilla's list of John's assets, not even affection was listed. She said John wasn't too much bother. He could play bridge, dance perfectly, ride a horse well and he could make intelligent conversation. He was an ideal escort.

Lemon wondered if Renata could make intelligent conversation and if she would be a handy convenience? She wouldn't have to ride the pinto.

Lemon became aware the game was over. Renata was discreetly jubilant! The bid had been a grand slam. She was filled with triumph. Bubbling. She was charming. She said to Lemon in soft exuberance, "Did you see that trump fall? I thought it wouldn't!"

An opponent groused with good humor, "You had me from the beginning. You finessed that spade perfectly. It was my only hope."

Lemon smiled at Renata's delight and didn't comment. He hadn't seen anything or known anything about the game except that he was where he could see her and had had the excuse to watch her.

She laughed at Lemon. "How can you be so calm? We did it!"

"You did." He was honest. "You were brilliant." Of course, he'd have thought her brilliant if she'd scuttled the whole shebang.

She bubbled on, looking at him and smiling that big smile under her hand-tousled hair. She was simply mush. She told Lemon, "You trusted me. You sat so calmly, so confident I could do it that I just had to figure it out. You were wonderful!''

Lemon blinked. He nodded courteously. He congratulated her. He did and said all the right things. And he understood that she'd thought his silent, mesmerized, X-rated thinking had been confidence in her card play? He wondered how she would react if she'd known what he'd actually been thinking?

As they rose to change partners, she said earnestly to Lemon, "You never gave me any advice and you didn't come over and hover over my shoulder. You gave me such confidence. Thank you."

"You didn't need me."

She was honest. "I would have welcomed your advice. You were very kind to trust me."

How could he spurn her feeling that he'd given her confidence? She thought he'd trusted her when he hadn't even cared? He wanted to be honest and tell her how little he cared about the game. But he could not. It might rob her of her triumph. He said it again, "You did it all by yourself and you did it perfectly."

With the next two partners, the cards dealt to Lemon couldn't be beaten. As the other three separated to move to their next tables, Renata said, "See? I needed your luck."

He'd risen to hold her chair for her, and he replied seriously, "You don't need anyone else's luck. You hold everything." She did. His attention. His libido. But she was talking cards. Who gave a hoot in hell about cards?

She laughed, "I hold ... everything?" She shook her head in laughing disbelief. "I held one trump."

Lucilla was especially aware of Lemon's attention to Renata Gunther. She insinuated herself into Renata's attention, but Renata was only polite. She was cool to Lucilla.

So then Lemon was interested in seeing to whom Renata responded with warmth. And he noted the ilk of people who caught her regard were rather conservative. Was it possible that Lemon Covington was lured by a conservative woman who followed rules?

He decided he wasn't that lured.

He was attentive to Beatrice Martin when she partnered him. She was lovely. She had all the equipment a woman needed in body and mind, and she used both well. She flirted. She smiled.

She responded well. Not as well as she had earlier, when he was still solvent, so the rumor of the fall of the Covington fortunes, which Lucilla had spread so quickly, had dimmed Beatrice's enthusiasm. But she still viewed him with some intrigued interest. She would probably consider a dalliance.

With him labeled as poor, it wouldn't do for Beatrice to get involved with a loser. However, Lemon knew Beatrice was old enough and experienced enough that it would be interesting for her to briefly comfort him. He knew his reputation as a lover was exaggerated and mostly made from the whole cloth. He wasn't as experienced or as jaded as was thought.

She was so kind that it was apparent she thought it must be very difficult for a man who'd had such means to be left with nothing. She thought his card house was collapsed. She could be kind. It would be the humane thing to do. That was how she would justify such a thing.

Lemon didn't mind.

However, Pots appeared to be interested in that one. He made it pretty clear to Lemon that he was to back off. To underline the fact, when Pots was dummy, he came over to their table and told Beatrice how to play her cards against Lemon. And he'd been right.

Pots got out a cigar and stuck it into his mouth. Beatrice and Lemon both said "No!" at the same time. Lemon said "The ladies," which was warning enough. But Beatrice said, "I can't stand cigars." And that did it.

Pots considered the still-wrapped cigar and then he slowly reached over and slid the nasty, quite thick cylinder down between Beatrice's nice, round breasts as he said, "It kills moths."

She left it there. That was calculated, and Lemon was impressed Pots had taken such a chance. So that was how that wind blew? Pots was staking out Beatrice?

Why not? Silas was considering Lucilla, John had Margot, and Lemon Covington was the odd man out.

But the "odd man" was lucky in cards. Lemon couldn't lose. It was a weary, irritated man who relentlessly won in his own house at a game he only tolerated because other people took it seriously.

With men, the greater lure were professional sports games, hunting and poker. If women were included, it was bridge.

In order to know and entertain women, one played bridge or had dances. They would dance the next night. The staff would temporarily clear away the chairs and tables, and the band would play until midnight.

The women would dress up and look beautiful, sparkling with jewels and pretty dresses and flirting. The men would flirt back and tease as, on another level, they talked to other men of other things.

And Lemon decided it was all a stupid waste of time. Living, playing and making a living. Being a do-gooder, interfering in lives, spreading money and ideas around. Learning how the given money was filtered through other hands for "expenses," leaving less and less as it all but disappeared before it arrived where it was needed.

He thought of all the rip-offs. Of trying to help people who only wanted more-than-enough . . . easier. Listening to gi'mes quarreling and holding protests because they were expected to help themselves. What good was there in any of it?

Burnout. Lemon recognized it. Running cattle could do that to a man. It seemed so fruitless to work so hard with something that didn't want to do what you wanted it to do. Cattle would rather live free, in their own way, and not end up on somebody's table. Simple.

Why was he sitting at a table with people who didn't have anything else to do but meet together in order to pass time?

Ah. So. What did Lemon Covington want? At thirty-five, what was it that made him so restless and dissatisfied? What was making him so critical and sour?

Lemon was damned if he knew. Those people were almost all good citizens who worked their tails off trying to construct organizations and businesses that would employ more people for better money, and incidentally making a bundle themselves before giving it away for tax purposes.

Lemon sat there and played bridge. His thoughts ran along in disgruntled discontent. His clever mind kept track of the cards already played and speculated on who had those left. His mind plotted for whatever ruse would lure those holding the cards into misplaying, and he won again. How boring.

He leaned back, his arms folded, still at the table where he'd started. Everyone who paused chided or applauded him for his skill. And it was a skill of which he was not proud. It was just a skill. Easy. It meant nothing to the one who could do it.

That wasn't unusual. There are many people who disparage their natural talent.

Lemon won that first session. They all congratulated him, and he was courteous.

Renata was flush-faced and sparkling-eyed. He figured she was probably too strictly raised to be pliant and have an affair. If she'd cooperate, she could give him a sense of challenge, of winning. She was probably selfish.

The guests went out onto the brief lawn and wandered around, sipping wine as they stretched their legs and bodies after the first session of the tournament. It would be continued the next day. Some changed clothes and swam in the pool, playing, making the serious swimmers give up and either play or leave the pool.

Women are seldom serious swimmers. Those swimmers would be out the next morning early and swim laps. Renata would probably be one. She would be courteous to whoever spoke, but she would be serious about swimming.

Lemon wandered around, avoiding being snagged into any group. He was looking for her. For Renata. She was at the fence talking to the pinto. She still wore that multibrown thin, soft afternoon dress. She looked like a wood nymph.

Lemon went over to her. He hadn't run over. He'd walked pretty naturally. He said, "Careful, he can bite."

"Poof," she retorted, smiling at the horse.

Lemon noted her cheeks were a little pink. For a horse? Or because he was there? Just the idea that she might be aware of him caused his sex to tingle down its length. If a woman's blush was enough to quicken him, he was hard up. And he put his hands into his trouser pockets and smiled over his thinking.

"He's a darling."

Women tended to say things like that about a horse that simply looked like a horse.

The pinto snuffed and shook his head. But his eyes showed white. Lemon went over and took the horse under his chin and told Renata, "He's not a pet. He's a real nuisance. He can bite or pitch or trample or do any number of sneaky and nasty things. Lucilla is the only one who can ride him and have him behave."

Renata said a deflated, "Oh."

"I paid good money for this horse, and I keep him around just to remind me that looks aren't very important."

She said another soft, "Oh."

Then he looked down at her and said seriously, "I'd kill him if he hurt you. I don't want you hurt."

Her cheeks pinkened again, her eyes danced and she smiled.

She was just fortunate that he was civilized enough that he didn't let go of the horse, lay her down on the ground and take her right then. His face was very serious. He let go of the horse and guided her out of horse-teeth-reach before he put his hands back in his pockets.

She looked back at the horse as she put a hand to her wind-teased hair, and she said, "He really seems like a darling."

"All males are like that with a beautiful female."

"Are you being deliberately darling?"

And totally serious, he replied, "Yes."

She didn't reply or flirt or tease. She continued pink-cheeked, and she watched him.

He'd never experienced anything so erotic. That seemed impossible. He'd had eager women do all sorts of wild things to garner his attention. How could a blush or a silent, still woman drive his libido this crazy? It did.

He cleared his throat and asked, "Would you like to see the barn?" Why had he done that? A barn was a barn. That was all that it was. If he took a woman down to see the barn, the hands would think he'd lost it.

She looked beyond him and said, "Sure."

"Have you ever been in a barn on a rainy day?"

She looked up at the cloudless sky and said, "Nope."

She was young enough to say "nope?" He was out of his depth. He only knew older women. He was getting older. Younger women were a whole new species. Was he becoming a lecher?

She looked around and asked, "Which way is it?"

Which way was...what? Oh. The barn. "This way." And he decided he would kiss her. Along here some-where, he'd manage to kiss her. He would.

His breathing changed. He parted his lips to breathe more silently. He couldn't scare her with harsh breath-ing. His body suggested they just go ahead and scare her, but he had more restraint.

She was somewhat animated, and she turned and commented in such a way that he was suddenly aware she was conscious of him. While he was intensely quiet and careful with his movements, she was animated and sassy. She was interested in him.

He took her into the barn and there were several of the residual men trying to rig a winch and having a time of it. There was no kind way to tell them they were in his way. He asked, "What's the problem?"

Being used to only having other men around, they weren't sure of the words that would come out of their mouths with a lady right there, so they mostly gestured.

Lemon led Renata out of danger and went up into the barn rafters to see what was wrong. Two of the men went up with him and they figured it out. It took a while. He never was entirely distracted from her presence. That was interesting to Lemon. He knew where she was every single minute, even as he helped figure out why the winch was being so balky.

Finally they solved the problem, and the men began to winch the bales up onto the top loft. Lemon went back down the ladders and watched that as he then returned to Renata. He walked to her, knowing exactly where she was, without ever really looking at her. He stood beside her and continued to watch.

She said, "How'd you know what to do?"

"I have a hard-nosed father."

"What's that got to do with knowing how to make something work?"

He looked at her finally, and she was just like always. Distracting. He was going to kiss her pretty soon. He replied, "He saw to it that I solved every single piece of equipment we had."

She smiled. "You were good friends."

"Not right away. I generally broke them first."

And she grinned at him, her eyes dancing.

She was a treasure. My God, he thought. She was a treasure! And the idea scared him.

Four

————

Lemon's realization, that Renata might very well be a genuine treasure, made him cautious enough to reconsider the urge to kiss her. Well, he didn't dismiss the possibility, but he did postpone it.

In his accumulated years, Lemon had been directed by his father to pay attention to couples. He was to watch and listen to other people. As his daddy had mentioned, getting married was easy. The only way to a full life was to find the right woman.

The kind of woman who wanted to marry a wealthy man, who pushed for it quite willingly, might not be what he wanted.

A woman who was the treasure of a man who realized what he had, knew she would take all his extra time and attention. Men knew that. The marriage in that case depended on the man's priorities.

There were ambitious men who deliberately chose women of the right echelon to marry, so that she would breed their children. That accomplishment took little of the man's time.

Such a man could be financially indulgent to the woman, while his attention was on what really interested him. She wouldn't distract him from the things he wanted to do: his business, male gatherings, politics or his other women. A man who was indifferent to a woman could use her as a shield or an excuse.

Unhappily, some women loved such men and only gradually learned they had never been sought out for love. While only being indifferent to her, the husband said to others that his wife was a great mother, a devoted charity worker or a wonderful hostess.

The saddest was the woman who made excuses to herself or others for the indifferent man. He was busy, he had too many responsibilities, he shouldered too many things.

It took a long time for a trusting woman to understand how she had been used. She'd waited too long before she realized he would never change. She then had to silently deal with her inner grief at her betrayal. Generally she had been married young and had no real training in working to support herself in the quickly changing business world. So she continued in her marriage, not realizing she still had options.

Lemon had seen such women.

He had then looked at his parents' marriage and understood they were not only lovers, they were good friends. They shared their lives. He remembered asking his mother, "How did you know you loved Daddy?"

"I asked that question with all the other boys who came around. Mother told me, 'You'll just...know. You won't have to ask. The only time that you'd ask,' she said, 'is if someone is appealing but you don't love him. Not really. With your daddy, I didn't need to ask.'"

"Do you really believe that?"

His mother had replied, "I suppose the rest of the yardstick is to figure why she loves you, or if she does? You can only be sure of your own heart. Don't let it blind you to her greed or boredom or indifference."

That's what Lemon's mother had told him, long ago. And suddenly, Lemon remembered the two years John Brown had loved Lucilla.

At least Lucilla hadn't married John.

But what about Renata? He'd just met her. How many words had they exchanged? He'd acted like a novice fourteen-year-old, and she'd responded in a very mature and kindly manner. He'd probably blown any chance he'd had with her.

But she'd been thrilled to be his partner at bridge, and she thought he was mature enough to've trusted her to play the hand by herself. She'd thought he'd trusted her and had confidence in her, but he'd only used the time in lascivious daydreaming while he could watch her face without upsetting her or anyone else.

Lemon couldn't snare such a treasure as Renata. He hadn't the time to cherish her as she should be. Of course...she had her degree. She was independent. She was sassy and exuberant. He could have an affair with her.

Yeah.

He would see if she was old enough to taste an unobtainable man. It would be a learning experience for her.

The experience would give her a coating of élan. It could make her look more carefully at—another—man.

Why should the idea of her looking at another man make a Lemon's mouth feel sour?

Although Renata had to be more than twenty-five— if she had her degree and was again taking classes—she was as green as a newly hatched chick. She needed him to help her be confident and to grow into adulthood without doubts as to her self-confidence.

She didn't appear lacking in basic self-confidence. But he could help her. From the very beginning, he would be clear that their coupling was simply platonic. Yeah. Play for him and tonic for her. That old saw.

Was he really that drawn to Renata? If he remembered correctly, when he'd first come down the stairs that very morning, his stare had been drawn to . . . Beatrice.

To be lured by two women in one portion of one day should be something to slow him down to some serious thought and a whole lot of caution.

But if they were cards in a game, he could discard one for a superior card. What was different? All of life was a game of chance. One only needed to recognize which was important and discard what was not. That covered just about anything.

He was probably getting restless because he was thirty-five and still unmarried. He and Pots were the last of their family. Two real gems. Maybe the family ought to let go of perpetuity. Some genes weren't worth the trouble.

Hers were.

But why would she want his genes mixed in with hers? She didn't. She was standing there in the barn with her hand on that dumb dog's head, watching two men showing off their muscles and lack of fear of heights as they winched bales of hay up into the rafters of a barn.

Well, it didn't take much to entertain her.

She was curious.

If he got tangled up with this treasure, he'd spend the rest of his life sorting and searching out things for her to watch or taste or see or think about. It would be a bloody chore. It would be interesting to watch her response. It would be interesting for him just to watch her...to know her.

He asked her, "Do you like raw oysters?"

She kept her eyes on the slowly lifting bale, her sweet lips parted, and she replied, "Ugh."

She didn't like raw oysters. Just think how he would have felt if he'd gone out on the rough greeny gray seas in a lowering, cold, dark storm to find oysters for her, come back to the house and have her not even *look* at them, but just say "ugh." That could dampen a man's wanting to please a woman.

She said, "Put your shoulder behind my head, my neck's getting tired."

Well, maybe a man didn't have to go out in a boat in a rough sea under a lowering gray sky. He could move over a half foot. Lemon did that. Her head fit into its place on his chest, right by his shoulder, just right. Her hair smelled nice. She had a freckle on her right cheek. He touched it.

She moved her head a little to keep the bale in sight.

His tender voice a little husky, Lemon said, "You've got a freckle on your cheek, right there."

"Baloney."

She needed some better responses. A man couldn't get all wishy-washy over a freckle and call a woman's attention to it to have her say Baloney. No romance there. She probably didn't have a soul.

He said, "I like these little curls around here." He put his big fingertip along her scalp line by her ear.

She said, "I think that bale's going to drop. Be sure the dog doesn't bolt."

If they were in a house together, and he'd built a romantic fire in the fireplace and turned out the lights, she was the type that'd come into the room, exclaim how dark it was and turn on the lights. She'd say it was too cold to sit on the floor with him in front of the fire. Her soul was a vast, empty plain.

She said, "Your shoulder is just right." And she turned her head a little, rubbing it against the front of his shoulder.

His heart filled with pleasure, his muscles expanded, his smile was mushy and his brain was flooded with purple.

She said, "There, they got that one." She swiveled her head to look up at Lemon. "Wasn't that scary? I thought sure it wasn't going to make it. If it'd fallen, the bale would have burst."

With her that close and looking right into his eyes, his tongue didn't work making words. It wanted to taste her. He closed his lips and smiled a nothingness, while he kept his errant tongue behind his teeth, inside his mouth. How would she feel if his tongue suddenly popped out to taste her?

His sex mentioned another way of touching. His breathing picked up and his sensitive body shivered inside because she was so close to him. He hadn't felt that much awareness since he was about ten and Sally Lou Phillips had taken off her panties.

He'd been hiding from Potato Head in the dunes on Padre Island. With Sally Lou's disrobing, Lemon had stayed hidden, quite riveted. Sally Lou had never known she'd had a witness to her first nude swim. Sally Lou had been four years older than Lemon. She had been very... different.

He looked on down to Renata's chest under the soft shadings of brown material and found her concealed form quite lovely. Very feminine. He put a hand on the other side of her waist and didn't do anything else.

He looked up at the men, who were now wrestling with the hoist again. He said to her in a husky, manly manner, "I'd better help."

But as he began to withdraw his hand from her waist, she said, "No, they have to figure it out for themselves."

So Lemon suggested, "Do you think it may be our watching that has rattled them? Do you suppose they're trying to keep you here so they can show off for you?"

That obviously was something she hadn't considered. "Surely not. Maybe you ought to let those boys go into town more often?"

He licked his lips to hide the smile and stop a guffaw. "Now why would they go into town?" And he waited for her obvious reply.

"They're lonesome out here?"

"For..." he encouraged, "what?"

"People!" She gestured. "Someone to see. It must be lonesome out here with—are there only three or four men holding the fort with the others gone?"

"There's the house crew."

She scoffed. "The house crew never associates with the barn people or the cattle people. *And* vice versa! In the echelons of work, the people are more snobbish than you apparently realize."

"They all seem courteous enough."

"You pay them."

"I mean in helping one another. We had a fire in the far barn? All the crews from all over the area pitched in and worked well together. A whole barn was at stake, and they saved it! It was an achievement! And the sweaty, dirty people all cheered and laughed and hugged and slapped shoulders. It was nice to be a part of it."

The two men had gotten the next bale aloft. It had been even trickier, but it shouldn't have been. They were showing off for her. Lemon had known that with the second tricky bale, and he'd allowed it. He wanted her there in the barn with him, with her head using his shoulder and his hand on her slender waist, his three bottom fingertips touching the top of the forward curve of her hipbone.

He asked, "Would you like to see the water hole? That's where we mostly swim. It's more interesting than the pool."

"Why is it... more interesting?" That was a logical question.

He replied readily, "We don't have to skim it or put chemicals in it to clear out the scum, the tree leaves don't block the filter... and we skinny-dip."

"I've never—"

"What?" He grinned knowingly.

She amended her words. "I've always worn a suit."

So it was with some conviction that he urged, "You need the experience. It will be such freedom that you will always remember where you were when you did it... first. We can come out here tonight, when nobody's around and it's dead dark. There'll be no moon.

And you can splash and frolic to your heart's content." He added nobly, "I'll keep watch for you."

She grinned and bit into her lower lip as her eyes sparkled. "Tonight?"

"Yeah." His voice was clogged somehow.

Faintly, in the distance, the dinner gong rang once.

Her eyes widened and she exclaimed, "I haven't changed."

He said, "We'll run."

They took off, with Lemon suiting his steps to hers and the dog loping along quite easily. Her body trembled and shimmied in such a way that it was just a good thing she knew where they were going and he didn't have to figure it out.

They went in the back door closest to the barn and up the back stairs and down the hall.

She gasped, "I have to shower."

He stopped and appeared surprised. "Why?"

"I'll smell like the barn cats?"

He crowded her carefully as he put one hand on her back to hold her steady. He sniffed around her head in a way that caused extraordinary shimmering reactions in her body.

His, too. He assured her, "You smell wonderful."

She wasn't convinced. "You live out here with cattle and horses and dogs. Your nose is not reliable."

She went inside her room and unmannerly closed her door. A selfish woman. He hadn't even had the chance to offer to scrub her back . . . or anything else. He went to his own room, stripped and rinsed off and redressed to be back in the hall in time . . . to wait.

Finally, he tapped on her door gently and received no response. He turned the knob and the knob did turn. He hesitated, then opened it a bit to call, "Renata?"

There was no reply. He frowned. She'd fallen in the shower and hit her head and was unconscious? He opened the door and called more clearly, "Renata?"

No reply.

She was dead. He would spend the rest of his life in regret if she wasn't somewhere on this earth, and he could even just *think* he would see her again. He would— And he wondered how that idea had settled into his subconscious? That was spooky.

He looked hurriedly around the room and went to the open bathroom door. She wasn't there. The room was empty. The bath was empty. Everything was tidy. She was gone!

He recalled Margot's report that John had watched the aliens land last New Year's Eve. They'd just returned? Returned and taken Renata! How could he get where they had her?

He went down the stairs to find her at the table, looking for her place card. He went to her to tell her, "You're next to me."

"How do you know?" She looked as if she'd never been in a barn in her life, and her dress needed more top. Any man there could see that her breasts swelled beneath the fragile cloth and the gaping neckline was too low. There was a deep shadow between her breasts as they touched.

He said, "You need a jacket. It's cold this time of year."

"It's July. We've had a scorcher today. Your house is perfectly air-conditioned. I'll be fine."

He nodded noncommittally and showed her to her place, to the right of his. He seated her as he inquired, "Have you figured what sort of subjects you'll initiate, in order to coax me to speak?"

"I understand Beatrice will be on your left. She'll think of something. She's never been without something to say as long as I've known her—since I was a child and she was in her final year of college."

His laughter was caught by his teeth biting into his lower lip, but his eyes were filled with it.

He took Beatrice's card and exchanged it for another down the table a way. The woman who then sat to Lemon's left was a ponderous political person who had world opinions and quotes for anything. She was matched by the man to her left, the man across the table from him who sat next to Renata, and the women on either side farther down. It was a long time before the silent Lemon and Renata could leave the table.

As that was accomplished, Lemon led her to a discreet stairwell and said, "Go up and get a towel—discreetly, of course—and I'll meet you right here at the bottom of these stairs. Okay?"

"Why do I want a towel?"

"To swim!"

"I'm freezing."

"That's the air conditioner. Some clown—" He. "—turned the temperature too low. Outside, it's a steaming July night."

"I'm not sure I have enough nerve to do this. I probably ought to be familiar with the pond before I try night swimming."

"There's nothing to it. We'll go down and you can see exactly what it's like. You'll be fine. I'll be there to guard for you. And I'm a senior Red Cross lifeguard. I'll take care of you."

She did hesitate. He smiled his smile used for irate bulls or rabid dogs or hesitant women.

She said, "Okay. We'll look." She turned and went up the stairs so she missed seeing what sort of smile the one he was using then became. Had she seen it, she wouldn't have come back down.

But she did.

He was waiting restlessly, hyped, his mind going a thousand miles a minute. His laboring support system was on overdrive. He said easily, as if with some surprise, "Oh, so you're going to swim."

She glanced at him cautiously. "I'll see."

They went out very quietly, and Hunter picked them up right away. Lemon said, "Hello, boy."

Hunter gave him a patient glance and then smiled at Renata.

She briefly put her hand on the dog's head, but then ignored the animal.

He trotted along beside or in front of or behind them.

Lemon stayed close to Renata. He looked at her and smiled. She considered him. He was different. He was probably similar to the pinto. Lucilla had said the pinto could clear fences when he learned why there were mares. John had been astride the horse at that time and was given credit for the pinto clearing the fence.

The fence hadn't been one of the barriers for the show, but a real fence that was high enough to keep stud horses away from the mares. John said he'd tried to keep the pinto from going over the fence and had lost the tussle. Ergo the horse had gone over the fence, and willy-nilly, so had John. John said he did brilliantly just staying in the saddle.

Lucilla could make the pinto go over the gates on the course. She was the only one. Any male would do whatever Lucilla wanted.

Renata looked over at Lemon. Lucilla wanted
Lemon. Well, she'd wanted him until it became known
that he was probably broke. His house of cards was
tumbling. How strange it didn't seem to trouble him
that he could lose this house and land and all it held.
Maybe he hadn't assimilated the disaster or maybe he
wasn't stable.

If he had lost everything, would he behave? A man in
that position might do something he'd never consider
under other circumstances. What more could he lose?
He might not care. He might be more aggressive or he
might not listen if she would protest.

She stopped and looked around.

He went a step farther then looked back at her. She
was so quiet as she turned her head, looking around. He
smiled and said, "The land is different at night. Listen."

She could hear sounds. A dog barked at some distance.

Lemon said softly, "That's old Dutch. He's just
talking. When he's serious, the sound's different. Did I
tell you about Dutch meeting Hunter? Hunter wouldn't
give an inch, and Dutch was stopped in his tracks. It
was interesting to see."

She asked, "If...Dutch...had lost his position, what
would he have done?"

Lemon had no idea she was comparing him with a
dog. He replied honestly, "I think he would have ad-
justed to being second and would have been a good
right-hand hound. He's a good dog, but he isn't relent-
less about it. He could take being second if the other
dog could prove himself better. He's a good dog for a
pack."

"And you? Could you take being poor? If your fortunes crumble. Can you and John figure a way for you to keep Cactus Ridge?"

He was a brief time assimilating her words because he kept forgetting he was supposed to be on the down slide. "We'll be okay. There's no problem."

"Denial never works."

He rubbed his face to erase his smile and walked a step or two. And he realized his fake disaster was all that had made her easy with him. He had her compassion. Now, how was he going to reassure her without lying? "Don't be afraid for me. We'll be all right."

"I do hope so. You have a wonderful attitude about all this. Most men would have been frantic. Are you this calm because you've never had this sort of thing happen before now?"

Uhhh. "John is superb. He'll figure a way. He says it isn't as bad as I thought."

"I'm so glad." With compassion, she touched his arm.

She'd again touched him voluntarily. He resisted with all his might and striving not to crush her precious body against his and kiss her right then. It was a stunningly heroic effort. In a blurred voice, he said, "You're very sweet."

She said, "I can see you quite clearly."

He smiled. "I can see you, too."

"You said without the moon—"

He lifted his head back and his brain whirled around searching for something, anything to solve this irritating observation.

"You said no one would be able to see me skinny-dipping." She turned and looked around. "Through the trees, I can see the house quite clearly, the barn, the

fences, the trees, and even from here, I can see some of
the pond. Its surface is smooth. Anyone in it would be
reflected by the stars. I can't go skinny-dipping tonight."

"Uhhh..."

She turned and started to go back to the house. The
dog obediently turned to follow. Lemon's tongue kicked
in finally, and he said, "Well, that is good. This way,
you can see if anyone should come along and you could
duck down. You'd mostly be underwater anyway. But
you could see as well as anyone around. You couldn't
be surprised."

She stopped her retreat and she did consider.

Earnestly, he said, "The fun of skinny-dipping is the
swimming. You'd be all underwater. Not just standing
in it up to your knees but being clear down in the water
with just your nose out. It's the feel of the water on your
bare skin that's—" he had to breathe and swallow before he continued "—so nice."

"I'm not—"

"Come look. It's a distance. You can see all around
the way. Come see if that's not right."

So she did turn back, and she did walk along beside
him, with him sneaking quick peeks trying to judge her
willingness.

The dog also turned back and went along, walking
around them, nearby, over there and back again.

She asked, "Does Hunter know the word g-u-a-r-d?"

"I don't know. I haven't had him long enough to find
out." He simply accepted that Hunter would stay
there...for a while.

"I wonder why the dog decided to stay here with
you?"

Lemon was indignant. "Don't you recognize me as a superior man?" He huffed, and she laughed. "If a dog can see it right off the bat thataway, why can't you?"

"You hambone."

"When Hunter chose to stay here, I felt ten feet tall and very humble all at the same time, but, Renata, he won't stay with me. He's still looking for someone. Did you see him walk through all the people, looking? He's lost someone."

And Renata made a sound in her throat. It was compassionate. It was a sound to heal a man's soul. How could he convince her that he needed healing, too? No. It wasn't healing.... How could this happen so quickly?

By then she was standing on the bank of the pond and looking around. It was screened by new mesquite growth and the bunches of cacti. The grown mesquite trees shadowed the moon with their tiny leaves of lace.

The dog drank from the pond.

She said, "I've never swum in a dog's drinking bowl before."

"It proves the water's clean."

"Ahhh."

She sounded as if she acted in response to wisdom.

Lemon observed her in that location. They were in a faraway place. It had once been a savagely contented place. It had been iffy and wild. And he understood she would have coped.

That slender, fragile woman was strong. If she wasn't willing to try a new experience, she wouldn't be out there with him.

She might be cautious, but she had adventure in her. And she was curious.

Renata was different from any woman Lemon had ever known.

Five

Renata looked over the creek-formed pond, which reflected the starlight. The pond was about a hundred fifty feet by ninety. The outline was irregular. The trees around it were taller, as are most which are near water. There were some thick, short cedars with rough bark and limbs with scant greenery. But mostly the trees were mesquites.

Between the mesquites, Renata noted several happenstance paths which were enough for any observer to see if there was someone in the pond, if they just looked. While the entire pond wasn't visible to any position of observance, any active swimmer could be noted by the pond's disturbed surface.

Renata turned her head to observe Lemon and said in a lofty manner, "A dog drinking from the pond is no proof the water is pure. I've seen dogs roll in the most—distasteful things."

Readily agreeing, Lemon replied "Them there's huntin' dogs? They do that deliberately to disguise their scents? They roll in the vomit or excretions of what they're following."

She again said, "Ugh."

Lemon considered the fact that she needed a wider vocabulary. He could teach her all kinds of words. Not those. Tender ones. He told her, "Men do similar things when they hunt. They try either to lure or to disguise their own scents. How do you like my after-shave?"

She replied instantly, "It's so strong that it just about knocks me off my perch."

He moved back. "I'll jump in the pond." He'd said the words right away so those were his tongue's automatic response, but his cunning brain noted that she realized she was the canary and he was the cat. He was going to get her.

He smiled like the tomcat he was. But he was disturbed to find a portion of his conscience wondering if he was being fair to her. Maybe she didn't want to be had by him. Hell. He'd have to spend time with her, endangering his own emotions as he made sure she could be willing. She just wasn't the impulsive, sudden type.

But... maybe she was!

She'd just met him that noon—only eleven hours ago—and she was out there in the bushes with him, in the dark, away from everybody else. She probably...trusted him? She trusted him! Damn. No woman should put the burden of trust on a some-time man. She was not only trusting, she was stupid. How did she know he was worthy of trust?

He asked her, "Why are you out here in the dark, wandering around with a man you hardly know?"

"I know all about you, and you promised to see to it that nobody peeked in the dead of the moonless night when I went skinny-dipping. You said everyone should experience such an adventure."

He nodded the entire time she spoke.

In chiding, she mentioned, "You didn't mention the stars."

He looked up at the billions and billions of TEXAS stars. The stars in TEXAS were always closer and bigger. Standing in their light was very like being in a room with a billion candles, except it wasn't that hot. It was a wonderfully balmy TEXAS night...just right for skinny-dipping.

He looked around. "You can see there's nobody, nowhere, no how. You can shimmy out of them there rags and hop in."

"Rags?"

He readjusted the words. "Glad rags?"

She was primly sure, as she indicated her clothed body in that elegant gown. "This is a statement."

"What's it say?"

She lifted her nose and looked down it at him. "That I don't need any help."

Speaking of the ranch hands, he warned her, "If the barn cats saw you, you would." Then he accused her, "You never pulled those straps up but just let your dress hang off...your shoulders in a shocking manner."

She looked down at her chest in some surprise. "This is perfectly decent."

He growled, "Where?"

"Here. On me."

He scoffed. "You hardly have on any top at *all!*"

"No one stared." She was uppity.

"How do you know that?"

She shrugged in a delicious way that turned his head clear around or made him dizzy. The reaction was so similar in disorientation that he couldn't be sure which had happened. Since his spine still worked, she had probably only dizzied him.

"How do I know?" She repeated his question with another. And she explained kindly, "I looked around."

"Naw. You were polite and kept your attention on the people around us who were arguing politics and stuff."

"I also gave my attention to them." She licked her lips in a studied way before she said gently, "They may have needed me for checking actual fact." She turned her head, showing great talent for doing something like that so cleverly.

He complained, "And you hardly ever looked at me."

"Of course I looked at you."

"Not enough."

She retorted, "Phooey."

"You have the damndest selection of responses I've ever heard tell. You need other words."

She was prissy. "Like..." And she lifted her eyebrows with studied courtesy. She was a tad sassy.

Her response was so delightful and flirting that she made him a little breathier. He supplied her with a selection of suitable words as he moved his hand in circles to indicate the choice. "Darling, of course, yes, right now. Those kinds of words."

"Baloney."

His reply was in elaborate indignation, "There's another!"

She looked around in quick alarm. "What? Where?"

"No, no trouble, except for you. You say Ugh and Baloney and Phooey and stuff like that there, and it annoys me. You're supposed to be kind and gentle with me. You're supposed to be wide-eyed and impressed with anything I say."

"Because you're broke?"

In exasperation, he declared, "Because you're female!"

She considered that. "Aren't your rules out of date?"

"Not likely."

Following his advice, she was kind, and she explained gently, "You're still talking fifteenth century? We ladies have progressed somewhat since the British women—in that time—marched on the House of Lords asking for female rights."

He commented thoughtfully, "You're too young to've been there."

Being precise, she explained, "Antonia Fraser wrote of that, using letters from those years."

Lemon labeled the writer, "She's a meddler in men's affairs."

Renata didn't protest, she just said succinctly, "I...see."

He was suspicious and asked cautiously, "What do you 'see'?"

"You're one of those kind."

"What—kind?"

She again practiced looking down her nose at him, and in the starlight and shadows, she was superb. Beautiful. Perfect. How could he know that this soon? Well, he'd known her for over eleven hours.

She was still on their subject and replied in a snooty manner, "You're a male chauvinist male."

He shook his head. "That's an outdated comment? Women don't say that there no more, no how."

She protested that bunch of words with a heartfelt "Good grief."

He sympathized. "Don't be sad. I've done things that were out of style, too, and it's okay. But I'm not a male chauvinist. I'm a new man. I share. I'll share this pond experience with you. Take off your clothes and let's..." He stopped.

She waited.

He said hoarsely, "I'll turn my back—over there in those bushes—and I'll watch out for you while you go ahead and experience one of life's other pleasures."

And darned if she didn't inquire, "What...other...pleasures?"

He said earnestly, "I'll explain another time. Not right now. Not this very minute. But there are some...other things...you should experience...with me."

How many times had she heard something very similar, all along the line? Since she was—what—fourteen? No. There'd been Joe D. at ten. Yes.

Men either assumed it was up to them to educate every female or to check out what she knew so far. Some were hilarious, some clumsy and some a real tussle.

Renata looked around. Maybe it would be wiser to go on back to the house and forget this pond for now. She could gather a bunch of women tomorrow night and try it out en masse.

Maybe not. It would be more exciting to try it alone in the night, discreetly, knowing he would be able to hear her splashing around...in the pond...totally naked.

He moved away several steps. "Call when you're through swimming. Don't just get dressed and leave me here all by myself, still watching." That is what he said. And people thought foxes were sly. He added, "I'd hate to roust all the guys from their beds to search for you and have you up there in your nest, innocently sleeping away while we dredged out the pond."

She didn't laugh out loud. She said kindly, "Thank you for this secluded adventure. You're really very kind." She may not have laughed out loud, but her smile was suspect.

He responded nobly, "Glad to oblige." He turned away, then called back over his shoulder, "You know not to dive into unknown water? Wade in."

In her scanning of the area, she'd noted the perfect spot to disrobe and go into the water. It was a couple of huckleberry bushes. There were no thorns like the nasty ones on the mesquite. No sweet mesquite beans to draw ants. It was dense with leaves and just right.

He called softly, "Are you in yet?"

She replied, "Just about."

She'd just slid off her shoes and set them aside. Heels were only good for level ground, walks and floors. They weren't for adventuring out and around.

One thing about that long dress, the lining was attached to the gown and she wore no panties. She slid it off and hung it on a huckleberry limb. That wasn't "...a hickory limb...." as in the poem, and she fully intended to go near the water. She'd be swimming in it in just another minute.

She hadn't expected the mud.

She tested the bottom, wading ankle deep. What if the whole pond was...ankle deep? She drew back into the huckleberry bush and called, "Lemon, where can I dive in?"

Having watched the dress come off from her huckleberry-shadowed, star-outlined form, he was clever enough to ask instantly, "Where are you?"

"By the huckleberry."

"Which one's that? Wave an arm out in the stars, I can't see you in the shadows that way." He lied.

"You don't need to see me. I'll just wave the arm." She did that and there was no reply. She questioned, "Lemon?"

"We never dive off the side of the pond. I forgot to mention that when I told you not to dive in. It doesn't get swimmable until you get away from shore."

It seemed his voice was closer than it had been, but water can bounce sound. She hesitated. "Where is the best place to go into the pond?"

"Here."

She looked over her shoulder. He was right *there* and stark naked! Beautiful. She said a discreetly smothered "Eeek!" and went in a running-churning into the water with a splashing scramble, knowing instantly that was the wrong thing to do. She surfaced out in the middle of the pond and looked back. He was nowhere aro—

He surfaced right beside her and laughed.

She said "You beast!" as she shoved a palm of water at him.

In a spooky voice he told her, "I'm not that wimpy Lemom Covington, I'm the Creature from the Black Lagoon. He owes me his life, and every year he has to bring me a nubile female so that I may vent my maddening lusts."

"Every year? In July?"

"Yeah. I come in heat only at this time every year. That's why he allowed the bridge tournament to be held here. He had to lure unsuspecting females for my pleasure."

"Well, darn. He flubbed up. He should have brought you the one named Lucilla. She would have been perfect for you."

"In what way?" the Creature inquired.

"She's as strange as you. You would understand each other. She would have submitted willingly to you for the treasure buried in this pond over the centuries."

"So. You know about the treasure."

With her wet hair down in snakes on her shoulders and her eyelashes spiked by the water, she was simply gorgeous in the starlight, and not at all discomforted. She told the Creature, "Of course, you would have a treasure. It's logical you would have some lure. What can I forfeit, without giving my body to your horned member?"

"Ahhh, you know about that, too."

"Everyone knows about you. Women talk."

"A bunch of busybodies."

She laughed softly, but the water magnified it. "Go away and let me swim. If you don't, my host will do you bodily harm."

"I'm your host."

"No, Hunter is. He's right there watching, and all I would have to do is call to him, and he'd eat you alive. I'd escape with your treasure and you'd be only a pile of chewed bones. If you consider the consequences, you will realize you'd be wise to quit threatening me with mayhem and go away so that I can swim in peace. I'll send out Lucilla just as soon as I get back to the house."

"Did you ever see the movie about me?"

"Yes. That's why I know that although you're strange, you're really very kind. You'll not insist I do anything rash. You'll save me from yourself."

"Damn."

"You have a wonderful imagination." She grinned at him.

"I was raised by a mother who, in her formative years, had saved all the 1930's Flash Gordon comic strips. She apparently never noticed the drawings were lightly pornographic."

"She hid them?"

"Grandmother allowed her to keep them. Mother's reading never was censored. She gave the strips to me. She loved the drawings. She thought the imagination was wonderful. That's what probably led me to playing Dungeons and Dragons in college."

"I heard that was mind altering. Boys got weird with it."

"Naw. It was great adventure. When Apple began to make personal computers, it was us that became the first hackers."

"Aren't hackers the ones who break in on the computerized files and steal them?"

"Those are crackers. Hackers were the leading edge of expanding the use of computers. The first telephone linkup was a wondrous thing. My folks could afford mine. There were kids that were stymied at first. Now we have Prodigy, Genie and CompuServe. But I still have hacker friends from that early time. They're all a little strange and it tilts me if I'm with them too long. Their minds reach farther than mine."

She laughed softly and turned to move away, swimming leisurely.

He swam nearby, keeping track of her and the area. Hunter was on the edge of the pond, watching them both very alertly and moving along to be close to them.

When she paused to tread water, Lemon said to her, "Hunter swims. I told him to guard you. Did you know that when you threatened me with him?"

"No." She lifted her arms and tilted her head backward into the water to straighten her hair.

For the briefest glimpse, the tight tips of her breasts were revealed so quickly that it was almost not at all, but only a dream of seeing her. He was frozen by the idea and with his arms out resting just below the surface, and curved, he hung in the water, mesmerized by her.

Thirty-five years old and hypnotized by the idea of seeing a female body? What was happening to him? One body was very like another. There weren't any surprises.

But she was different.

She was kind, she was bold, but not to him. She wasn't flirting. She was just...with him. And she hadn't teased or lured him. She was treating him as if...as if...

As if she could handle him.

For a roving man, his age, who'd been around the block a time or two, that was somewhat irritating. His voice a little throaty, he mentioned, "You're flirting with something very serious here."

"No. I'm experiencing one of life's little adventures. You recommended it. You said you'd guard me. I take you at your word."

"Why are you being so careful to keep me at arm's length?"

"I've evaded determined men for some time now. I'm the last of my line, too. You at least have Pots for back up. I have no one. No cousins, no one."

He sighed with exaggerated melancholy and gave up. "I suppose you want me to make it legal and us have twelve kids to start up the families again?"

"No. No. You no longer can afford to do that."

Slyly, softly, he asked, "And if John gets it all straightened out and I'm solvent again?"

"I might...consider it." She grinned at him.

A water nymph. One from the times of the gods. She'd been sent there to lure him in and use his human body, so that back on the mountain she could discuss him with the others. Sure.

But she was a goddess.

Moving her arms just a little, opening her knees to lie froglike in the water, she watched her companion. His imagination was a wonderful surprise. That he could tease and not touch, that he could seem so safe and still be naked in that pond with her. He was crafty and probably dangerous.

She inquired, "After you sell everything off, would you still have enough left to educate the twelve children you mentioned?"

"John would figure a way."

She commented, "Twelve is a boggling number."

"Ten?"

And she laughed, so softly, so amused. He wondered if she always laughed softly, or if she was conscious of their isolation and didn't want to call attention to them.

In the night, a woman heard laughing the soft amused way she did, would make any distant man's ears prick up and his curiosity would also rise.

Lemon glanced at Hunter. He was looking around and listening. A remarkable dog. Lemon turned his attention back to the goddess. She, too, was looking around and listening.

Rather dreamily, she commented, "It's just exactly as you said. This is magic. However, I really hadn't planned to share this experience."

His reply came immediately, seriously, in profound instruction, "Sharing always expands an adventure. You look around more in order to comment on more things. You're competitive."

"How could you know that?"

"I watched you play a grand-slam hand."

"I was doing that to prove to you that I knew how to play bridge."

"I already knew."

"How?"

"As you mentioned about women, all people tend to talk."

She scoffed and snorted, saying the impossible, "About...me."

"Yep."

"What?"

"That you secretly wear a garter belt that's—*gasp*—purple!"

She almost sank. She didn't say the words, but around the gulp of water, she actually gasped, "Who told?" And having hung peacefully, barely moving in the water, she then thrashed around to stay afloat.

He reached out and took her hand, stabilizing her. And she was aware that he'd found her hand and hadn't fumbled around on her body.

He told her, "I can keep a secret." He was totally asinine. And his soft laugh was deep, husky and very wicked.

She smothered her choking with her hands. He offered to pat her back. She shook her head.

As she settled down, he mentioned, "It's just a good thing I came into the pond. You'd have drowned."

"Don't be silly. I wouldn't have choked if you hadn't come in here and mentioned my purple garter belt."

"Why... purple? I like red."

She assured him loftily, "It won't make any difference."

"I realize any color of garter belt will hold up your stockings, but I prefer red."

"You'll never know."

"Don't count it out."

She commented with interest, "That's another of the sports references in conversation. Count out is boxing. Countdown is nuclear." She settled down to dog-paddling as she went on, "Out in left field, row, time out, tackle, home run— Where would we be without reference points? It must be difficult for an alien to sort the words. There was a man from Guatemala who commented on the words bough, bow—to bend—bow tie and bow and arrow. That bow being spelled like the bow. Tree limbs and people limbs. Car tire and exhaustion tire. Ours is a confusing language."

"I saw MacNeil's English language series on PBS—"

That did surprise her.

"And in one part, he was saying all the words that came to England from Norwegian marauders. The simple words we use are just about all from Norway.

The French contributed their share . . . like river. It was an interesting series."

"The shadings of words are marvelous. Honesty and integrity. It isn't the same. Yet if someone is honest, you believe he will pan out. Pan out is from the gold rush?"

"Likely."

"You said that deliberately."

"'Course."

"We all know TEXANS are different and speak strangely."

"I reckon so. The whole entire kaboodle."

She hid a smile and added, "More than likely."

He looked up at the stars and mentioned, "We had a hard case that whupped his horse."

She scoffed. "Now wait a minute. Hold on there. No fooling?"

His eye crinkles were obvious in the star-reflecting pond water. "No doubt about it."

"That's mighty strange."

He shrugged. "There you go." Then he added, "It don't get no better'n this."

She laughed in her throat.

Her laugh curled his fingers and toes, lifted the wet hair on his head and straightened out everything else. It was a sound that a man wanted from a woman's throat before he got serious.

He said, "I think I'm turning into a dried-out prune in—"

"How could you be dried out in the pond here?"

"This is dry TEXAS water?" That was the do-you-understand questioning statement. "It shrivels you. You've probably aged ten years wallowing around in this here liquid dirt."

"Glory be!"

And he had the guts to reply, "Shucks, ma'am, I'm just a po' TEXAS boy."

She lifted her arms and took handfuls of her hair as she muffled her shriek.

And he laughed down in his throat in the perfect way that touches low inside a woman.

Little squiggles ran inside her body, and she recognized them as alarming to her. They signaled danger? No. It was different. It was desire.

She said, "I believe I agree that we've been in long enough. You go on out of the pond, and I'll stay just a bit longer."

"A tad."

"Ummm-hmmmm." She smiled like a lorelei.

He said calmly, "If you want to feel a part of the universe, you oughta turn over on your back and float as you watch the stars. You'll know what the astronauts felt, floating in space."

She almost did that. Then she remembered she wore no covering but water. She said, "You go along. I'll wait until you walk away, then I'll do that."

He paused just a minute before he assured her. "Watch Hunter. I'll call him away when I've left. When he leaves the pond, you can float on your back and experience this marvel. It'll be worth the effort."

He hadn't expanded on the worth. He just went with effortless, silent strokes over to the shallow water. He turned and accused, "You're looking at me, woman!"

He was beautifully male. His muscles and body were shadowed by the starlight. His eyes, his hair, his lips. They were altered by the starlight and he was still a marvel.

Without commenting, she slowly turned her back.

Behind her, he said a soft "Damn."

She smothered her laughing reaction, but he heard it over the water.

She listened as he walked away from her in the water. He was taking care to minimize the sounds. Then there was silence.

She paddled around, looking into the bushes and trees and down the open paths to other places. There was no— There he went. And Hunter turned his head and watched; then he looked back at her, looked around the area and trotted off in the direction where Lemon had appeared.

He was no longer there.

But Hunter went.

She was alone.

She rolled over on her back and lay still. Her ears were underwater and heard only the water sounds. She looked up at the sky and it was magic. She was in space. All those suns. There must be people or creatures on at least some of the planets out there. How would they ever know she watched? Who, there, watched the billions and millions of suns and wondered if there were other thinking creatures...somewhere. It was amazing.

And nearby, among the trees, that viper Lemon stood, his lips parted to silence his heavy breathing as he watched her lying on the water, barely moving, her appendages loose, her knees slightly bent and her heels apart as she floated. Her hands barely moved as she stabilized her body and kept herself from drifting.

She was in the stars. She was of them. She was a magical being. How had she come there? How could he keep her? How would he keep her...there with him?

He was going to have to deal with his foolish declaration to Lucilla about being broke. How was he going to do that?

His eyes never left the semisubmerged figure in the pond. Her hair floated in odd ripples around her head. Her face and breasts and knees were all that could be seen above the surface, he considered that here was a woman worth looking at a second time.

And he'd only known her since noon? He looked at his watch. Twelve hours. He began to remember all he'd learned about her as a woman in that short time. He felt there could be no surprises after this strange day. He knew her mind, her humor, her honor.

She was special.

Six

It was strange that Lemon didn't kiss Renata goodnight. All the way into the house and up the stairs, he considered it very seriously. And he mused on the fact that he was anticipating kissing her. He couldn't remember when he'd last felt that way.

He'd never had to. Women willingly kissed him. He had to guard himself. Some women were very aggressive. Around the Covington fortune, there were women who didn't hesitate to indicate interest. Kissing had become an automatic reflex ... for some time. When had the anticipation of a simple kiss again become thrilling?

Was she thinking about kissing him? He was intensely aware of her. He helped her up the stairs, supporting her elbow lightly on his hand. His hand was excited to touch her elbow. Now that was weird. What was so salacious about her elbow to excite his hand in that way?

As they walked down the hall toward their rooms, she smiled up at him, almost causing him to stumble, and her sweet lips told him, "The pond is exactly as you said. Thank you for the wonderful experience."

She thought swimming in a pond was a wonderful experience? How would she react to—

They had reached their opposite doors. Would she consider which they'd use before she suggested his room was larger?

To give her an excuse to delay leaving him, he said, "Breakfast is at eight."

She nodded and smiled a little. She cast him a nothing smile and said, "Good night." And without hesitating or hurrying or anything but being as natural as she could be, she opened her door. She'd smiled up at him as if he was just a man. She went into her room... and closed the door... gently... ordinarily.

He stood there in the hall.

As intimate as they'd been, naked together in the pond, she wasn't ready to be kissed. She hadn't stopped at her door, turned to him and lifted her mouth. It would have been a natural thing for her to have done.

She'd treated him as if he was only an acquaintance. She'd smiled over her shoulder at him and was... pleasant.

After sharing that intimate swim... and he hadn't touched her body. He could have, easily enough, when she was thrashing around, but he had not.

She ought to have known that he was attracted. With all the willing women there at his house, he'd been out in the dark with... her.

Did she *expect* such undivided attention? *All* of the
host's attention? For the entire evening? She'd seen him
change Beatrice's card with another—the political
woman—and she had to realize then that he'd put her
next to him, to his right, in the place of honor.

Maybe she thought he was honoring her for making
the grand-slam bid and playing it perfectly.

Perfectly? He hadn't noticed whether she had or not.
He'd been watching her interesting face and thinking
five X-ratings about her body.

She could have said, "Your room or mine?" She
didn't have to just go on into her own room and leave
him standing alone in the hallway with people walking
around him like— They hadn't been alone in the hall?

As he then recalled, the hall had been packed with
people chatting and calling to each other. He hadn't realized that was so while she'd so gently closed the door
of her room. He did remember nodding to several
comments as he then went over to his door.

And he remembered several shadow people pausing
as he'd passed in front of them when he'd crossed the
hall to his own door.

No wonder she hadn't offered to kiss him.

Renata Gunther was a stickler.

Ah, but everyone who saw them would know they'd
been swimming. Her hair was down and still wet. Her
makeup was gone. She'd been carrying her shoes. No,
she'd put them on at the bottom of the stairs.

But her hair had obviously been seriously dunked.
She'd been swimming. With him. Everybody would
know.

That rumor would probably go around as fast as his
being broke. Well, maybe not quite that fast.

She had been swimming. And she'd been all that time with him. How easy she was with him. How natural. How fascinating.

Of course, there was the actual pool. The other guests would probably think they'd been swimming in the floodlighted pool and not the starlit pond. But they were both back in evening clothing. If they'd been in the pool, they'd have had on their swimsuits and robes.

He stood with his shirt half off and looked vaguely in the direction of a corner of his room. What about her was so fascinating? And his mind began to go over their time together.

Other aspects of his efficient mind allowed his movements to go on taking off his clothing, showering, brushing his teeth and getting into bed.

By then the X-rated part of his mind had come to her shadow disrobing in the huckleberry bush. And his dreams of the languid turnings of their naked bodies in the pond water were very different than those gentle memories which had actually happened.

When his alarm went off the next morning, Lemon was still in a fog of bemusement. He smiled at nothing and got obediently out of bed. He stretched wonderfully, feeling the strength of his good body, and he looked fondly at the disarray of the bedclothes.

He stripped the sheets and mattress pad from the bed and put them down the laundry shoot to the basement. Because of all the guests, he made up his own bed. The household staff would be stretched in spite of the extra help hired just for the weekend.

He again showered as he shaved with the shower razor. Then he dressed and looked at himself in the mirror. His blond hair was thick and so light colored he'd gray well. When that time came. Some long time yet.

His eyelashes were sun bleached and his eyes were a dark blue. He thought he was a real nothing.

While he wasn't malformed, he could have been better looking. For Renata, he should resemble one of the Olympians instead of looking like the Creature from the Black Lagoon.

He stared at himself and thought he seemed to be a man who'd become too experienced about life, men, business. Crookedness. Disillusion. He gave another thanks for John Brown.

There was a discreet knock on Lemon's door. Lemon called "Come!" And his face became vulnerable as he suddenly wondered if it would be she who opened the door.

No. It was John.

Lemon went on tying his tie loopings as he said, "Good morning, John, what brings you out this early?"

John replied patiently, "The next time you impulsively want to discourage a woman, consult with me on how you should do it, okay?"

Lemon looked fondly on his friend. "Trouble?"

"It might take all the reserve fund set up at the bank to salvage L.C. Partners, L.P. There's a run to recover the investments."

"Pots?"

"Naw." John chided his friend. "You know Pots. It's mostly the little investors. They want their money while you still have some cash."

"What have you told them so far?"

"To wait for the six-month financial statements from our certified-public-accounting firm."

"Good." Lemon nodded. "As I recall, we do have a clause in the agreement that no interest is paid in the first year?"

"Right. We set up the reserve to cover anyone who wanted out during the first year."

"I'm sorry to put this additional burden on you, John. I just—"

"You've never been a burden. You're a sharp man with wild ideas which generally work. The reserve fund should cover these nervous withdrawals. If it should go beyond that, we shouldn't have to use the bank. We can use the cash back from that spent oil well you managed to lure into being young and frisky again. God only knows how you knew there was another pocket of oil in that rusty, misused, discarded well."

Lemon shrugged. "A hunch."

"There's probably enough in the reserve fund to cover all the little guys. If any of the big guns get restless, we'll have to juggle, but we still shouldn't have to borrow from the bank."

Lemon looked at his friend. "If there's anything I can do in this mess I've caused, tell me."

"It's not a mess." John's smile was rueful. "It's a challenge. It is just a tad inconvenient. The premise is solid. Don't forget that you gave me a hundred shares of the Partners stock."

"You'd earned it, setting it up. I'm sorry rumor has made it seem to be sour. It was a chance for some friends to make some cash. I regret the ones who could really use it are the ones pulling out. They should have come to you first."

John shook his head. "As long as you were lying, I wish you'd told her you were terminally ill, instead."

Lemon shook his head. "Uh-uh. She'd have jumped at the chance to hold my hand and lay a cool cloth on my burning forehead—until she could be my wealthy widow."

John laughed. "You're right."

"Since I'm not expiring, she isn't interested. However, John, I need to mention that Renata Gunther would have nothing to do with me until she learned I was going broke."

"Ahhh."

"Only the sound? No comment?"

"She's worthy."

Lemon laughed with such exuberance.

"So." John walked some steps. "You aren't anxious to hold a meeting and soothe the fainthearted jitters?"

And succinctly, Lemon rather theatrically enunciated, "No."

John sighed dramatically as he elaborated, "And you'd rather I leave this whole shebang up in the air and find a miracle solution to whatever and however?"

"I've always said you were brilliantly perceptive."

John warned, "This could tarnish your business acumen."

"But it should enhance yours."

Quizzically, John asked, "You don't mind?"

"Seeming to be a little dense can be an advantage on occasion."

And John remembered the rattlesnakes in San Antonio who had tried to get at Lemon's money. Lemon hadn't been fooled from the start, but he'd been fascinated by the pitch. During the presentation, Lemon had stayed lax and friendly while John had stiffened.

Lemon was a better man than John Brown. He smiled at Lemon and said, "I'll be careful not to betray your sneaky method of getting acquainted with Renata."

"It was also done to escape the claws of that witch who bemused you for two whole bloody years!"

"I hear!" John held up his hands as if to ward off a bee assault. He smiled at Lemon. "I happened to be going through the files and found a vague reference to a deal that included Lucilla. You bribed her to get her off my neck."

Lemon corrected, "Actually, I freed her of your obsession."

"By bribing her?"

Lemon was serious. "By coaxing her to let you go."

"I owe you." John's voice was soft. It was an emotional time.

Lemon said seriously, "Save me from this mess, keep those investors, and your debt is free and clear."

"I'd have done it anyway."

"But being a business major and a stickler, you'd have felt the burden of obligation. This way we're both relieved of this mess. And John?"

John looked at Lemon with all his attention.

"I'd do the whole thing all over again to make Renata comfortable with me. Money can be a problem with some women."

"Not very many."

"That's why I need this chance to understand this particular one. Renata Gunther. She's unique."

"She swam in the pond with you."

"We didn't touch. It wasn't her idea that I get into the water with her. She treats me as if we are friends."

"You feel differently." It was a statement.

"I've never anticipated a kiss this much...in years." Lemon was still hung up on that amazing fact.

John guessed. "You kissed her."

"Not yet."

"Margot says she's a wonderful woman. Smart, alert. And she has humor."

"She's very tolerant. She doesn't fuss over Hunter, but he's her guard."

"Against you?"

Very softly, Lemon told his friend, "I haven't tried anything. I told you I haven't kissed her yet."

"Yet." John considered Lemon.

"Not yet."

The two men observed each other, but it was John who did the weighing, and he smiled at his friend, "Good luck."

Lemon replied, "We'll see." Then he asked John, "Could you give me a list of the people who want out? I might convince a few to stay in."

So John told Lemon who were those dragging their feet.

Breakfast was orderly. It was just a good thing the rooms on the first floor of that big house were so large. There were sliding doors between rooms, and the tables curved into open-ended horseshoes in both rooms. With the table openings each facing the widely divided wall, it made the tables seem connected.

Again Renata sat to Lemon's right. She smiled at him sleepily. A long wisp of her hair was down her back. It had been neglected when she'd put up her hair, and Lemon found it very erotic.

But then he found her sleepy smile erotic, her mouth closing over her fork was erotic, and the way she patted her lips with her napkin was wondrous. She breathed erotically. She turned her head and it was an erotic movement. He was in deep trouble.

Lemon had the kitchen staff come into the dining area, and the guests stood and applauded them. It was charming.

Breakfast had been stunningly delicious. The guests groaned and said their brains would be drained by their digestive tracts and they wouldn't know an ace from a two. That brought guffaws and snorts of disbelief.

Having snacked in the kitchen as he complimented the staff, Lemon returned to the table. There, he had pointedly eaten a half piece of toast with honey and smiled benignly.

As the guests moved sluggisly into the ballroom where the tables were waiting with their new decks of cards, pencils and score pads, Lemon found time to tell two of his guests, "Don't be hasty with the L.C. Partners, L.P. It's going to be okay. Listen to John. Wait for the six-month CPA statement."

Lucilla came along and waited to speak with Lemon. She said with interest, "You appear to have hope for your fortune."

"We're working on it." His gaze on her was cool; his face was serious.

"I'm glad."

He made no reply.

They settled down to play. The games were silent and intense. These were real bridge players.

With the midmorning break, Pots's friend Silas said quietly to Lemon, "I can cover for your L.C. Partners. It's a good investment. I'd be very happy to be in it, so count on me to buy up any nervous nellies."

Lemon smiled and replied, "It is a good investment. Thank you for the vote of confidence. I believe it's going to be all right."

"My word on help." Silas was serious and tilted his head to consider Lemon . . . to weigh him.

Lemon smiled. "I'm much obliged."

At another time, Pots mentioned, "I have some loose change if you should be in a pinch."

"Ah, Pots, every time I think you're useless, you do something like this."

"You're the only cousin I've got, and I have to think of the family reputation and solvency." Pots grinned. Then he sobered and said, "I mean it. Call on me."

Lemon told John, "I've had two serious offers of backing."

John said instantly, "Silas and Pots."

"Yep."

"They gave me blank checks."

"No!"

"Yes. I wouldn't take them. You have good friends. Renata offered to help. She doesn't want you to know that. She swore me to secrecy. I gave her my solemn word."

"I like a loose-mouthed man when I'm the only one he tattles to. Thank you for telling me."

"There are *some* things a man just needs to know."

Lemon regarded John soberly. "Lucilla took hers out?"

"She was first."

"You paid her off." It was a statement.

John's look was steady. "Right away."

Lemon nodded with some satisfaction. The words were said by a man who had been used by that woman. John only now had had his revenge.

Revenge.

We all have our Achilles' heel.

When the cigar smokers went outside to indulge their filthy habit, Lemon noted that Hunter went among them, checking again. The dog was a gem. Regretfully, he only tolerated his new master.

It was obvious the dog searched for a specific person. Had the man who had trained Hunter died in a wreck, as Tom suspected? No stranger to the area had encountered an accidental death. Not in the past two years. No one was searching for such a dog. Had the death been normal—at a hospital or at a home—the dog wouldn't have left, searching.

Lemon had had an additional, wider search made. There had been no advertisements for such a lost dog. Nor had there been replies to Tom's or Lemon's advertisements.

Lemon felt regret for the obvious fact that Hunter's new master was not Lemon Covington. How was he lacking? And Lemon felt some inadequacies.

Lemon saw Renata open the door. She came onto the porch and she stood glancing casually around. He watched.

She replied smilingly to those who spoke to her, but she continued to search the crowd discreetly. It was obvious she looked for a person. A man. Lemon began to study the gathering with some hostility. The loosely gathered men were easy and talking as they enjoyed their smokes or just the companionship. An unusual number of the men were not smoking.

With Renata on the porch, turning her head to see everyone there, some of the men became more animated. Some laughed louder. Lemon was disgusted with them. But he, too, wanted her attention.

He started for the porch and saw her as she saw him. Her face pinkened and she smiled...and she looked no farther.

She'd been looking for him!

The thought went into his heart and then out to all his various limbs, and he was thrilled by the idea of her hunting him. To be with him.

Or—

She wanted to save him from bankruptcy? Damn. Was that the reason she was trying to find him?

Hunter got to her first. He sat smiling up as she leaned over and spoke to the dog. Then she put her hand briefly on its head as she stood to watch Lemon come up the stairs. She smiled.

The dog moved back to her side and nudged his head against her thigh. She put her hand back on his head, and he was still.

Hell, Lemon could do that if she'd keep her hand on him. He teased her in a quiet voice, "You come out to smoke a cigar?" He pronounced it cee-gar.

She pinkened more and laughed softly, but she just shook her head.

He said, "Just now, I heard a rumor that the pond disappeared into the sand. I need to go check it. Would you come along as witness?"

"Of course. Do I need a camera or a notepad?"

He told her gravely, "No. Intense observation would be sufficient."

So they went around the house in a very quiet manner, and then off into the trees past the fence and the row of pecan trees his grandfather had planted as a young man.

They walked along quite normally. They were friends . . . male-female friends. She was safe. "It's still there!" she exclaimed.

So he looked into her eyes and said very seriously, "That just proves that rumors aren't always accurate."

She pinkened even more.

He said, "You will note that I'm wearing a more discreet after-shave? Sniff me and tell me your verdict."

He wasn't wearing any scent. He leaned to her, and she put her hand on his shoulder as she stretched up a little and took a step closer. She sniffed him.

So he did the only logical thing he could think of, and he kissed her. It was wonderful. It was mind-bendingly erotic. It wasn't enough.

Her body against him was altering his genes. It was the Dr. Jekyll and Mr. Hyde syndrome. He released her, put his hands to the sides of his forehead and his fingers sliding into his thick blond hair as he leaned back with his face to the sky and his eyes closed.

He was breathing so strangely that she put her hand on his arm and asked, "Are you all right?"

He asked crossly, "Why aren't you wearing a warning sign?"

She shrugged very prettily under that purple morning dress. She apologized earnestly, "No one's ever been susceptible to me."

"So you recognize the problem."

She mentioned helpfully, "You were all right last night."

"You didn't kiss me last night." He said that in a censoring manner.

She pointed out earnestly, "But we were in the pond together. We weren't . . . clothed, and it didn't bother you."

"As far as you knew."

Her eyes got bigger.

He frowned as he slowly lowered his hands from his head—which hadn't split after all—and he asked her with building tension, "Are you wearing that purple garter belt under that purple dress?"

She was as serious faced as he, and she replied quickly, "I don't believe I should mention that."

And he laughed. He stood and laughed as he shared their nonsense. Then he took her against him and said, "This could be very serious. If you couldn't be interested in me, let me go now."

And she said quite soberly, "Not yet."

"What's that mean? That you want more of a taste, you want more time to see if we match or you don't want to let me go...yet...but that you will."

"I want more time."

"I'm not sure I can handle much more of you."

"Are you addicted to women? You're very susceptible."

"And you're not?"

That boggled her. "To...women?"

"To men. To me. Even Hunter is still looking around, and that's after he gave up Tom to try me. Is that what you'd do, too? I'm not sure I could take three discardings in one weekend."

She asked cautiously, "Three?"

"A woman offered to marry me, the dog is looking around for another master, and then there's you. I am most certainly entangled in you. Is it all lust? I don't think so. I think you're something special."

"This is too fast."

He cleared his throat and said, "You didn't tell me if you like my new after-shave."

"It's perfect."

Not even the soap had an odor. He was without any false fragrance. It was all just him. She liked the smell of him? His ears pointed and he said huskily, "You ought to sniff around and see if I pass muster."

"Army."

He blinked slowly and turned his head as if to listen to the word again, and he said, "Huh?"

"Pass muster is army wordage contributed to our language."

"Yeah." He smiled. "Want to see if I—pass muster? I'll let you sniff any part of me that appeals to you—" he coughed a bit and swallowed and blinked "—if I can." With a foggy voice he elaborated, "If I can behave."

"Is there some problem?"

He saw that she was sincere. She wasn't on the same wavelength as he. He said, "You're not on the same wavelength."

"Why not?"

He said, "Wavelength is radio."

"Yes, but it could also be a space probe."

"Yeah." He considered that. "Are you leading me away from the subject?"

"Language?"

"Sniffing me."

"I'm not sure I should . . ." she began.

He said seriously, "I'll behave. I think I can."

"It's me that's the problem."

"Well, for a man to have a woman sniffing around on him, close and interested, it's a very potent thing for him. He's susceptible."

"I wasn't worried about you. You have wonderful control. I was thinking of myself. You make me feel a little dizzy."

"Now—" He breathed in carefully and was very still. "—that is serious."

"I agree. I've never had to deal with a reaction like that, and it scares me a little."

"Why does it...scare you?" His words were soft and careful so's not to spook her.

"I'm not sure what I might do to you."

"You'd harm me?" He was shocked.

"I don't think so. How sensitive are you?"

"Where?"

She gasped and said weakly, "I think I might faint."

He considered that, "I don't feel faint. I feel jumpy and intense."

"This analysis is driving me crazy."

"Talking?"

She was earnest. "Yes. Kiss me very carefully."

He scrambled her brains. He did that by taking her into his arms against his rigid, hard body and kissing her mindless.

She swooned.

He lifted her into his arms and carried her around. No particular place, just around. He liked carrying her. He said, "Whenever you have to walk, tell me and I'll get you there thisaway."

She lay inert, but formed the words with care, "People would talk."

"About what? Us being together?"

"You insisting on carrying me."

"But it's perfectly logical."

"You can argue any side."

He laughed. "I love you."

"It's too soon."

"Hell." He was reasonable. "It's been almost twenty-four hours. That's almost a month if we saw each other an hour a day."

"We slept in that time."

"True." He nodded sagely.

"We were not together all of that time."

He blinked. "You think we ought to sleep in the same bed?"

"You're shocking."

He reminded her, "You swam naked with me."

"I suppose you're going to rub my nose in that for the rest of our lives."

"If I do that, it means we'll be together."

She tilted her head and her eyes were large and serious. "Do you suppose?"

"More than likely."

He carried her to a discreet back door, and they straightened themselves in the cloakroom. Then when she asked if she looked all right, he kissed her again.

It was some time before they settled down and could be comprehensive again, and they finally went to the ballroom to view the players.

The bridge players were just about finished with the morning session. They noted the pink-cheeked Renata Gunther and the sly Lemon Covington as they entered quite indifferently.

One asked, "Where've you been? We looked everywhere for you. The cook and one of the barn cats had to sit in for you all."

Renata wasn't working with a full deck. She questioned, "Barn cat? An actual cat?"

And a low, smoky woman's voice replied, "A very wicked male. He smiles just like a barn cat. Sly and knowing. He's got all the women wiggly."

Lemon *tsked* and said, "How shocking."

But the smoky-voiced woman said, "So are you. We've all wondered where you two might be."

"We were outside discussing nature's scents."

"Oh."

And he had the gall to ask the smoky-voiced woman, "Now aren't you ashamed of your wicked mind?"

"Disappointed."

Seven

Slowly, Lemon and Renata went quietly among the earnest bridge players until they came to the cook's table. She was completely absorbed in the play, so the errant pair didn't interrupt.

But the two did see the lazy regard of the barn cat whose name was Dan. Lemon nodded and bowed slightly in acknowledgment of the man's volunteer replacement for them. Dan's eyes brimmed with humor as he returned their salute with a discreet nod.

Dan cleaned up quite well and appeared reasonably comfortable in that crowd. Bridge players are bridge players no matter where they are. They're like artists or writers. Actually, Dan was very amused to be where he was.

Dan was a seemingly indifferent player who not only knew every card played, he knew every nuance of every face in the place. He was a great cattleman. Only once had his beeves ever bolted. Dan solved their problems before they became trouble.

Dan was that good at cards, too. Clint had taught him. Clint was the ranch's top dog who was off on holiday to some god-awful place of stress, delivering medicines or whatever. Clint couldn't sit still for a minute. He said it was because ranch life was so tame.

Clint had said that right after a bull had burst from the brush and gored Clint's horse and hit Clint's leg at the same time.

Having completed their social obligations to acknowledge their replacements, Lemon and Renata went on through the room and out the French doors onto a terrace. They wandered off down the way, hand in hand, and they disappeared.

At lunch, the absent ones' places were taken by the cook and the barn cat, Dan. There was no mention or questioning about the absent two...not out loud. There were some whispers. Several pithy glances were exchanged. Dan saw those, of course, and his eye crinkles deepened.

The pair thought they were so discreet and subtle. They lived in a bubble of time, separately from all the rest of the universe. The fact that Lemon hadn't noticed any of the other people around in the hallway the night before, was a good clue to their intense concentration on one another.

Renata's gown was a flowing lavender morning dress of the softest, sheerest cotton. With her dark hair swirled up and held by antique tortoiseshell pins and held back from her face with a wide deep purple Alice band, Renata was a drawing from an early nineteenth-century poetry book.

Lemon was especially drawn by that wisp of escaped hair that was down her back. That wisp was like a little flaw that the Moors deliberately put into their perfect tile works because they shouldn't be as perfect as God.

Walking hand in hand, Lemon told his love, "Do you have any questions for me? Ask me anything." Lemon knew she had gone to John and offered to help him through this "bad" time.

"Did you miss not having brothers and sisters?"

Lemon was surprised. Of all responses, he hadn't expected that. "Yes."

She sighed, and he watched her do that marvelous thing. She explained patiently, "That was an opening for you to elaborate on how important brothers and sisters can be to one's expansion of character."

"I had Pots. He was older, wilder, and an amazing character. He boggled me. I was never like him."

She looked off and her eyelashes called attention to themselves. "I had no one. Not even a cousin. Mother and Daddy died in a plane crash when I was eight. I had a very elderly, dry great-aunt who allowed me to stay in her dark, dusty, silent house."

He guessed, "You hated it."

"I loved it. I spent a long time being still and waiting for ghosts. It was a little disappointing when there was none. I wasn't bothered by the staff. I read all the books in my aunt's library. Well, not all of them, but her taste in books surprised me, and she didn't censor my reading. I read some startling books."

He smiled a little and his eyes twinkled. "Wicked?"

"I wasn't exactly sure. There was a whole lot that I didn't really understand."

He raised his eyebrows and his smile disappeared. "Until?"

"I'm still not sure about some of the things I read."

He lifted their clasped hands and patted hers. With amused tenderness, he assured her, "You've come to the right place. I can explain anything."

She was silent for a long time.

He walked along, contented. Well, not very, but being by her and holding her hand helped. No, it was torture. Sweet torture. He could accept sweet torture for the time being. Actually, his body was deteriorating. The fire in his boiler was burning all his cells. He wouldn't last very long, not this way.

He looked at her and anguished that she was such an innocent. If she was at all compassionate she would—

"I've watched X-rated films."

He grinned ear to ear and said, "Wo—"

"I still don't understand how it's done."

"Sex?"

She nodded little bobs. "You have total control. I believe you could explain it to me without getting upset."

Up...set. She thought being passionate was getting—upset. That was lower than Square One. "Who all have you asked?"

"Mother, who laughed and said, 'Don't worry about it.' That was just before they died. I didn't have anyone for a while. I tried my great-aunt, who said persimmoniously, 'That isn't something we discuss.' And I asked one childhood boy who didn't know either and worried about having to do it."

"No adult male?"

"I really haven't been around very many. I went to a women's college. There were wild groups, but I wasn't invited to join any of them. I wasn't noticeable. I was

raised in a convent. That is an eye-opener for a Methodist."

"How was that?"

"I thought, being a Methodist, that I was probably
going to hell."

"That bothered you."

She shrugged marvelously. "I accepted it."

"In what way?" He was somewhat intense. Some
girls go off the deep end with an attitude like that.

"No way. I just accepted it as my fate."

He shook his head in tenderness for the young and
isolated Renata. "Did you mention your fate to anyone?"

"The great-aunt. She said, 'Balderdash!' But she was
a freethinker, so I just thought she was doomed anyway, so her opinion didn't matter."

He laughed.

She was earnest. "With your losing your money and
even this place, would you like to move in with me? In
return, you could instruct me in all the things I don't
know."

"You'd do that?"

"If I went broke, and that's impossible because of the
Trust, I would— Of course, you still have your parents. They'll take you in. I forget people have families."

That touched in Lemon. She was so alone. How
could she be? "Do you have a job?"

"I edit poems for a literary publication. That means
the presentations are elegant, the paper is handpressed
and the ink drawings are exquisite, but they are not
making much money."

Lemon was feeling more and more unbalanced. What
did he have here? An isolated chick just tapping on the

inside of her isolating shell? He was going to be the one to lead her along the paths of sensual reality?

The very thought tightened his muscles and weakened his bones. How had this occurred? How was he to creep carefully along this sagging high wire? He was scared spitless . . . but he was not unmanned.

She said, "I've watched the afternoon soaps. They appear to like it. Sex—" she explained in an aside "—and I doubt they're actually. . . Well, actually. . . Really doing anything real." She looked at him to see if he understood her.

Soberly, Lemon considered that she hadn't been indifferent or aloof the night before as they'd swum nude. She just hadn't known any better. She hadn't been alarmed by his coming into the water naked, because she'd never been accosted, propositioned or lured.

His eyes narrowed as he wondered if he was the one being led. "You've had a lot of practice kissing." He slid a glance at her.

She brightened and pinkened and flushed and beamed. "Do you think so?" She was so pleased!

She shocked him. He inquired, "Who all have you practiced with? You don't have to give the names. Just the approximate number."

"You're my third male. The timid boy who was afraid he'd be asked? A boy at Miss Genevieve's dancing classes. He caught me in the hall. It was awful. He kissed me over the whole bottom half of my face. Ugh! And a timid editor in New York. I believe he was trying to be friendly. But I have practiced on my hand. And it wa—"

"Your *hand?*"

"Yes. I put my thumb alongside my palm and pretended it was a man's mouth."

"That's... all? Your *hand?*"

She became a little snippy and her lips thinned. "I didn't have anybody to ask to help me out, so I did that!"

"I never thought a hand kisser could be X-rated. You knocked my socks off."

She had to assimilate his compliment. "I—did?" Her voice squeaked up, and she began to smile.

"You ought not kiss any more men. You're too dangerous. If you feel the need to kiss, come to me. I can handle it. Another man might not be able to resist you, and you'd be flat on your back in no time."

"Knocked out?"

"Seduced."

"How come you can't do that?"

"You *want* to be seduced?" He was incredulous.

"Of course. Everyone seems to be doing it, and I've been left out. I'm twenty-five and I've never done it."

In his stunned condition, he mentioned, "I'm thirty-five."

She was shocked. Her words stumbled earnestly stressed, "You can't anymore?"

"Oh, yes," he assured her avidly. "Now?"

She looked around! She did. She asked, "Where can we do it?"

While her words were said in a normal voice, they rang like bonging bronze bells inside his head.

His knees got weak. But while his libido went into orbit, his mind realized she only wanted sex from him. She wasn't mesmerized by him, as he was with her. She was using him. Him! Lemon Covington, the great catch, was being used as an experiment by a woman who was... curious.

He lost heart. He was only a—curiosity. She thought him broke and vulnerable; therefore he was usable.

How could she?

He looked at her. She was aware of him and was conscious of the turn of his head, so she met his look and smiled. "I hope I'm not too inept. You will tell me what to do?" Her eyes sparkled, and she was eager.

No. She was only curious. He was so disappointed that he wasn't entirely sure he could—do—anything.

She put her hand into the crook of his arm and hugged his arm against her softness. She wasn't flirting or coaxing. She probably wasn't even aware that his arm could feel her soft breast.

She said, "I thought you might . . . kiss me . . . when you knew that I . . . wouldn't mind."

She . . . wouldn't mind. His soul groaned in agony. She had no soul.

He kissed her with great tenderness, holding her gently to his hungry body. His body wasn't as put off as his mind. He was a little offended his body would be so crass.

She moaned in her throat, and her breaths were broken.

She'd be easy. His hot eyes glanced around and his brain chided their hunger. His body was rude. It shivered with need and was vulgar.

He'd planned a gentle seduction with the tenderness of softly loosened flower petals. This was going to be a red rose smashing with thorns.

No.

He had control. He could control her. Their coupling would be as exquisite as— And he remembered their kisses. Out of control, devastating, shocking.

He cleared his foggy throat and said somberly, "We need to go slowly so that you can understand."

"Yes." She licked her soft Lemon Covington-reddened lips, and her eyes sparkled with all sorts of lights. She smiled at him and asked, "Where?"

And he remembered he had condoms in his wallet in his hip pocket. To mention that would make him seem crass, so he told her, "I have to go up to my room for a condom." He looked at her so that the seriousness of the word would sink into her overheated brain.

She blushed even deeper and licked her lips before she replied, "I bought one."

"Where?" He was stunned.

"Before I came here."

"Why?" He whispered the word, he was so shocked.

"I've heard of your reputation. I was going to try for you."

"You have it on you?" His eyes' avid stare went down her dressed figure. Where?

She blushed and replied, "There's a discreet pocket in my garter belt."

"You have on the purple garter belt under that lavender dress?"

"Yes." Her eyes sparkled and she smiled, but the blush was deeper.

He became dizzy. His breathing system clogged. He was unable to reply.

She suggested, "What about the huckleberry bush? It's quite private and no one would notice."

No one notice? Yeah. Sure. His mind skidded around probable places in a rather undisciplined manner until he again took control and said, "We'll get the convertible."

She was exuberant, "We're going to do it in a car?"

She was putting him on? Was this some sort of revenge of the feminist group? Was this real? Was she?

He needed to know.

His voice was almost normal after he coughed a time or two and cleared his throat. He only had to start talking twice before he said, "Come with me."

And she sassed and swished delightfully, "I fully intend doing exactly that!" She laughed low in her throat in delight and shivered his timbers with the sound. She then sobered just a tad and asked, "You will be slow enough that I can, won't you? I've heard men can be sudden . . . I think that was the word. I might need a little time."

"How many men have you approached in this way?"

She was startled and looked at him in surprise. "None. . . ." Then she grinned and acccused, "You're teasing!" And she laughed deliciously in a low and naughty manner.

While his mind was offended, his libido loved it and his face smiled back. His conscience mentioned the errant smile and his mind agreed, but his libido ignored his stern chastisement.

His libido? Its ears were pricked. It stimulated his glands, his nervous system, the fine hair up his backbone, all his muscles and his urgent need.

It shocked him. She was so willing on such short acquaintance that he was feeling—used. And he considered the several times he'd pulled just such an approach and the reactions of those women.

Well, having as much money as he had had probably been a stimulant.

He opened the side door on the garage and led Renata inside to the silent, waiting cars. The convertible was sitting on the far side. He led her there as she looked around without commenting.

Under that lavender dress, hidden inside a secret pocket in her purple garter belt was a condom.

She didn't look the type.

She was quite wonderfully animated. Her kiss-reddened lips smiled as she looked around, very alert and interested. She loved the convertible.

He helped her into the car and went around to get into the driver's seat. It was just a car. Wheels. Transportation.

He'd long ago outgrown such cars. He no longer wanted to be recognized or followed. She was still young. Did he feel old?

Not exactly. He thought he just felt . . . disappointed. He was expecting a real romance with tenderness and time-taking convincing. It was a surprise to find she'd sought him with a condom in her garter belt. That seemed so crass.

Well, *he* almost always carried a condom or five. A man never knew when he would have to defend his honor and his susceptible body from some voracious woman. That's what he'd always hoped. And now here he was with just such a woman. But she only wanted his body.

When women were used by a needy man, did those women feel this disappointment? The fact was that, at the time, release was all the man had really wanted. Any woman would have suited his purpose.

But Lemon wanted her to want him, and not just for the experience. He wanted her to care for and about him. To share the love. The . . . act of love.

She just wanted to be sure he wouldn't be too quick.

Along a two-rutted winding road, he drove her to a favorite place in the low hills. It was completely private. Looking off, away, a man could see forever in all directions. No surprises. Total isolation. He parked the car inside the three-sided horse shed, and it fit. The car was hidden.

She looked around with great interest and the wind teased around her as if it couldn't keep its touch from her. It ruffled her skirt, blowing up it and causing her hand to control the light material.

The wind touched her hair, but the band kept most of it neat. With frustration rampant, the wind teased the little curls around her face and that one forgotten longer one at the back of her neck.

She was unutterably charming. Just looking at her filled his empty heart to bursting. He'd known her for over twenty-four hours.

She finally looked at him, and he realized she didn't know what to do or how to begin. She was waiting for signals.

He went to her and kissed her. It was the same chaos. To control the impact enough, he only touched their lips. A wasted effort. The kiss was just like the others. The very same. It was a no-holds-barred disaster. He wanted to put her against the side of the convertible and ravish her.

While she was expecting his intrusion, even anticipating it, she had been clear in that she wanted it slow enough that she could experience it with pleasure.

He was going to have to wait. Self-discipline. All that trouble just to be patient enough to give her pleasure. He could do that.

At least she hadn't picked the barn cat, Dan. He was the wham-bam-thank-you-ma'am kind. She'd chosen a man who was patient and kind. He smiled at the restless neophyte and said, "Come inside."

Inside the cabin was one room. That separate little outhouse hadn't been a smokehouse, after all. The room was just about filled with a double bed. The mattress was bare. It wasn't new.

There were no curtains on the windows, and the bottoms of the windows came to the top of the mattress. The windows were not clean. Neither was the floor.

There were no pictures on the walls. There was a bare table on which was a phone. A cellular phone. Yes.

Was that so he could make some business calls while he waited for her to... She was somewhat disappointed. She considered the back seat of the convertible, but there was all that fishing stuff in the back seat. They'd have to clean out the car, and he could be distracted into trying to cast another kind of lure.

There was no place to... disrobe. She was stymied. She sneaked glances at him. He was going from window to window to stand quietly, looking out on the horizon.

Well, the mesquites were rather short, and from that height they didn't block his far view. Perhaps he couldn't see this far at one time, from one place very often.

How often had he been out here? How often had he brought a woman out here to make love to her on that bare mattress? And jealousy reared its ugly head.

She lifted her chin and turned as he walked over to the next window. He glanced at her and forgot to look out of that window. She was like a druidess about to lecture him on the place around them. It was a magic place. What would she tell him?

He told her, "My great-great-great-grandfather built this shack. It has been a retreat for us all when civilization got to be too much. He got this land from the Comanches. The Comanches chased him up into these hills, long ago. Apparently they never knew about the spring. They were surprised my ancestor survived. They were disgusted. They sold him this land as being no account.

"He built this house right away. He did that for a good reason. The spring's under the house. See? Here's a trapdoor. If the shack was burned, those here could go down in the spring well and survive. The land right around here is very fragile. No cattle are run up here. It's left alone. This is a precious place to the Covingtons."

She looked at the shack differently then, and she saw the age of the logs. It was so dry up there, the wood just about turned to stone? She looked at the relatively new mattress and wondered about the bedsprings. Were there any?

The outline of the trapdoor hadn't been even. Perhaps, long ago, they hadn't had the right tools to be neat.

To know how many people had been in that shack intimidated her somewhat. It didn't seem like a hotel room, where it always seemed new and you never thought of the thousands of people who had slept in it.

The cabin was personal somehow, since it had a family history. It might have ghosts who would disapprove of Lemon bringing a woman there for carnal purposes.

He was at the last window.

Then he went to a chest and took out a clean mattress pad, sheets and pillows.

She stooped and ran her hand over the mattress. It wasn't dusty. With such dirty windows, that was a surprise.

"One at a time, we allow the men three days up here as a retreat. We leave the windows as they are, on the outside. We don't particularly want anyone to know we are up here and watch the countryside."

She was silent as she thoughtfully helped with the bed. It seemed so deliberate to help make up a bed so that she could lose her virginity. It was so calculated.

He said softly, "To my knowledge, in these years, no couple has ever slept up here."

"You never brought any..." Her sentence trailed off.

"No. And the men who have come up here haven't brought anyone along. It's forbidden. This is a special place. We don't want it known that there is water here. See the keg? That is always filled, in case someone is lost and finds this place. But the trapdoor is covered. It's outline is irregular to disguise its purpose."

"You showed it to me."

"I gave you my trust."

She looked at him then, and he was serious.

That was when she saw him as a man with feelings and honor and thoughts. Before then, he'd been a personality. Now, she understood he could be hurt. He was attracted to her. She was using him.

With the sheets neatly settled onto the bed and the pillow slips on the pillows, she said with bright interest, "I would like to go out and look around. You can see so far." With animation, she moved her head as she looked out of the dirty window.

He recognized cold feet when he heard that. He smiled softly and replied, "We might ruin your shoes. Those are handmade, if I'm any judge."

"I can go get a replacement."

"Where? Italy?"

And she smiled. "Yes."

"We'll be careful. Or, you could go barefooted."

"I didn't notice the ground."

"It's dirt. There are paths to the outhouse and around the perimeter to look out over the land."

"I'd like to see it," she said with interested animation.

And her jumpiness just about healed his ego. She not only was beautiful and charming, but she wasn't bold at all and she was beginning to back off from this adventure in his bed.

He had some fence-mending to do.

He showed her the privy and how it worked. He showed her the hay in the open-ended stable. It was fresh. And he showed her that they could both go barefooted and survive. He had feet that were indifferent to rough ground, while her feet were picky.

He teased her, and she laughed.

When they came back toward the shack, she said, "Would you mind lying on the hay? I find that more appealing than the shack. I feel all your ancestors watching in shocked attention."

"My ancestors couldn't ever be shocked. When you're older and more blasé, I'll tell you tales that'll shock your socks off."

"How much older? An hour?"

"Why, Renata Gunther, you shock me."

"I just might."

He grinned and said, "I've been partial to hay since I was a tad, and hid in the barn to get away from my daddy. It smells clean. It's soft. And it's always where you can be alone. I'd like to be in the hay with you."

"I've never been in a haystack."

"I can make us a small one, right here. I'll see to it that you think of me every time you smell hay or feel it."

And she smiled.

Eight

Renata didn't shock Lemon. She stood and watched as he forked hay down from the shed's loft. Renata Gunther sure was willing, but she wasn't bold and she blushed. She undid her buttons with hands that trembled so that Lemon said with gruff tenderness, "Here, let me."

She dropped her hands to her sides and stood obediently still. Her head was turned down and her lashes covered her eyes as she watched his fingers undo her buttons.

His hands shook somewhat and they were a little careless against her exquisite softness. Her body was so different from any other woman's. How could that be? In the general forms of women's bodies, there were no surprises. No. Hers was different. Beautiful. Fragile.

As he tried to figure out the sailor's knot on her long sash, she said, "Maybe we shouldn't . . . just . . . uh . . ."

His heart stopped. He froze and he opened his mouth to protest.

She went on, "just…jump into it…this way. Maybe we should have some…preliminaries?" She looked up, and their eyes met.

Her pupils were enormous. She was beet red. Her breathing was erratic. She was getting cold feet. She would, of course, want preliminaries. The great majority of women needed them. Men didn't. He was going to be dragged through a knothole backward—maybe forward, point first. At his age, he was too old for frustration.

He shivered and sighed. Delay was something he'd never had to endure. He'd heard talk about this kind of problem when a hot man had a cooling woman.

Guys had said the best thing to do under such circumstances was to recite the math tables. Okay. But he found the multiplication table surprisingly nondistracting and had to go on to metric conversion tables.

With attention, he could do those. Not reading well, he'd memorized them to show that he could, to show that his brain wasn't sluggish. Memorizing had been good discipline.

So he stopped removing her now-loose lavender dress, and he hugged her very carefully. He was starting from scratch. He said, "You are so special."

That was an automatic response. He'd said that, on occasion, to the several women he'd had, and it had always seemed true. This time it was sobering. Renata really was special. She really was different.

He kissed under her ear and along her throat. His scorching breaths burned on her cool flesh. He hugged her and didn't move.

That allowed his body to concentrate on hers. How different a woman was made from a bony, almost entirely flat man. His hands moved gently in a coaxing exploration.

But his fingers and muscles were getting stiffer. His breaths were roughening. He was making sounds of his hunger. He scrubbed his hard hand down her stomach and his breathing became harsh.

He kissed her thrillingly. He was thrilled. She loosened a little bit. She put her hands on his shoulders quite timidly. She wasn't ready yet. He knew that.

He kissed her some more and he said words that came naturally to his clever tongue. He told her how wonderful she was. How beautiful. How wondrously thrilling. How perfectly she was made. How exciting her body was to his.

She accepted those words rather vaguely. She heard the desire in his tones, and she was distracted from his words because his hands were crowding her more private areas and moving rather personally, intrusively.

His hand pushed up under her breast, making the bulge of it lean over the side of his thumb and the edge of that flat, exploring hand. She didn't make any shocked sound, like a gasp, because he wasn't actually holding her breast. He was only pushing it up, and his palm was just on higher ribs which, until then, had been protected from any touch by the covering of her breast.

She could feel the bulk of his sex against her hip and it seemed rather shocking it was so... forward and that he couldn't at least be... a little more subtle.

He distracted her mental censure as he kissed her mouth in a squishy manner that was intensely provocative. She shivered and felt the thrills under her arms, into her breasts and sliding down to swirl in the bottom of her stomach in her...sex. She was aroused. The feeling was very exciting to her stomach and a little shocking.

His tongue coaxed her tense lips apart, and she was very conscious of the fact that his tongue then tried to intrude inside her mouth. Why would he do that? An upper persuasion to a lower invasion. Now, from where had that saying come? When had she heard it? Why had she remembered it?

She probably hadn't understood the nuance and locked it away in her subconscious until the meaning was known and she could evaluate the quote and discard it. Its meaning was now clear. He was kissing her as a preamble to sexual intercourse.

He appeared to be upset or stressed. He was hyper and trembling. His hands were unsteady. He was sweating and hot! His noisy breaths were like steam. His hands shook as they scoured along her body. His concentration was intense, and she felt she was riding on a disorienting whirlwind.

His attention was riveted on her, but he wasn't talking anymore. He was pressing against her one way or another and he was so concentrated—just on her—that she was breathless.

He had her clothing askew and his hands were getting more familiar. They were hot and hard. She liked what they were doing to her chest and...down there. It was especially nice when his hand rubbed her...down there. But her breasts were swollen and pushy. They vied for his attention, and she felt his hand on the apex of her legs, but she was distracted when his mouth captured her closer nipple.

The shock of his lips pulling her nipple into his hot, wet mouth and his tongue working her nipple against the roof of his mouth was stunning down inside the furnace in her crotch. He was fanning the flames that were burning in there.

She gasped and pressed against his mouth and against his lower hard hand, and she heard an agonized moan. She was startled to know that hungry moan was from her own mouth.

He lay her on the hay and that freed him from trying to keep them balanced upright. He could explore more easily the morsel that was under his mouth and hands.

She murmured, "This hay's rough."

Breathing fiery breaths on her wet breast and licking it with a lazy, lascivious tongue, he chided between licks, "You're not supposed to notice. You're supposed to want me so much, by now, that you're not aware of the hay against your delicate flesh. I ought to be distracting you enough so that you don't notice at all."

She countered, "You're on top."

"I like being on top." He released her and loved her gasp of protest. He took off his shirt, moved her aside and lay his shirt on the hay. "Try that."

The material was a fine lawn. "It's still stickery."

He lifted elegant, full, sun-bleached eyebrows and said, "My trousers are next."

She sneaked peeks as he stood and shucked the trousers. He put the trousers under his shirt. "Try that."

She pronounced, "The fly is bumpy."

Hoarsely, he replied, "So'm I." But he sat her up and eased her dress off over her head.

She lost some hairpins and scrabbled around finding them. "These are antique heirlooms. Real tortoise-shell."

So gently, he said, "And you use them? Shame on you."

"This turtle died long, long ago. They were marooned in the Gulf. They ate him and lived. They saved the shell because it was beautiful. It's like my grandmother's Russian otter."

"A pet?" he inquired pleasantly as he spread her dress carefully over his shirt, which was on his reversed trousers on the hay.

"Her coat," she replied, monitoring her hay bed's progress.

"I believe your slip will make this just right." He smiled at her.

"I really planned on wearing it. The whole time. Covering my navel. It seems rather crass to strip down entirely."

While he nodded in understanding her words, he assured her, "It's no big deal. I'll show you my navel. It's just like yours."

He pulled his undershirt up and pushed down the band of his shorts to show her his navel, with its marvelous decoration of patterned hair.

She smiled and put her hand on him. "You're gorgeous. Let me see you." While he was stunned motionless in excited shock and anticipation, she lifted his undershirt and ducked her head down to look up under it.

He was back to panting, but he helped her pull off the undershirt.

She said, "Beautiful," and smiled as she moved her hand over his hairy chest.

He said, "I like doing that to you, but you're bolder than I am." And he copied her wandering hand's movement exactly. But her chest dipped and swelled. It was more complicated, and the texture was smoother than his.

She leaned and suckled his flat nipple. Then she popped it free from her mouth and laughed up at him. "You're hairy."

"I'll shave it clean."

"No!" she instantly protested. "I like it this way."

And he laughed. His agitated sex thrust out against the material of his shorts. With bold intensity, he said, "There is more of me to see."

She considered the thrusts of power. "It seems dangerous. Look how it bounces around! How do I know it won't attack me."

"It won't. Gently, it'll give you great pleasure. I need to take off your slip so that I can see that outrageous purple garter belt...and the condom pocket."

Renata shared the probability, "I really believe the pocket was meant for cab money in case an escort was unmanageable."

"Ah. And if I become 'unmanageable' you expect to find a cab out here? Ah-ha! My proud beauty. You are in my power."

She put a curled hand up so that her wrist was between her breasts, and she made her eyes large and pitiful as she said in an insincere pout, "You beast."

"You can get more into that last word! Try it again. Lights! Camera! Action!"

And he took hold of the bottom of her slip, the top of which was crumpled around her waist. He eased the silken treasure slowly up her body as she rose to her knees and lifted her arms as the slip went up over her head...and off.

She sank back down onto the semi-made covering over the hay. There she sat with her knees together and her feet tucked to one side. She wore only her purple garter belt, stockings and the handmade Italian shoes, which were a black purple.

Her hair was in somewhat of a disarray, what with missing pins and disrobing. She looked like a tousled mermaid who was semicivilized. Perhaps semicorrupted would be a better labeling. She looked ready.

He asked, "Where is that pocket in the garter belt?"

And she showed him. One long finger pointed to the clever secret pocket in the center dip of the garter belt, but her gaze stayed on his face.

She watched his sun-bleached eyelashes close down over his eyes as his glance lowered to see where her finger pointed.

Below was the rich darkness of the covering of her female secrets. It was distracting his attention from the garter belt. He put a hand on the silken hairs and smoothed the lovely pelt, soothing her. His voice was clogged as he told her, "You are so beautiful."

She replied softly, "So are you." She reached out a timid hand and smoothed the hair over a ragged scar on his chest. "How did that happen?"

And he knew she wanted to delay. So he explained in some tenseness, trying to be casual and show his openness and willingness to communicate. He explained the scar. "That was caused by bob wire." He was speaking of barbed wire.

With the delay, she could be more curious. She touched him as she asked, "How did you get tangled up in bob wire?"

"I was checking fencelines. A rattler signaled my horse to move, and it was a sudden thing. I wasn't expecting it. The horse was so embarrassed."

"You were hurt."

"It wasn't nothing. I'm sure I have some other scars you might be interested in. I love the sympathy. This here's where I was hit with a whip and—"

"A whip?" She was appalled.

"Yeah. I got in back of a guy practicing with a bull-whip and backed too close."

"And this one?"

"That was a knife."

She was shocked. "Whose? Why?"

"I was young. I went into a place because it sounded like something interesting was going on, and I walked into the knife." He added in a remembering way, "I was surprised."

"I would think so!"

"I did stop the fight when I fainted. One of the participants was a hand at our place. He was bigger than anybody else there."

Lemon gave her time to assimilate all that. Then he showed her a scar on his forehead by his hairline. "This was when I fell off my bike when I was twelve? I was watching—something and ran into a stopped car. The guy was so mad at me that he surprised me. I didn't understand him until I was older and got the responsibility of people to worry about." He smiled at her.

"But you do?"

"Yeah. So I take precautions about the men."

"I mean, do you realize you're mortal?"

"Only recently. In these last two days of being around you, I've found I want to live forever." He moved to take her close to him, his shivering arms holding her with rigidly controlled strength, and he kissed her mouth in sips. He lifted his mouth from hers to look at her. "You're more beautiful naked than you are in clothes. You're a magical work of art."

She responded with total commitment, "I won't wear anything."

Earnestly, he replied, "Only when you're alone with me. You stay dressed the rest of the time. You hear me? But when you're with me, you strip down to that garter belt."

She frowned with prissy impatience, "What *is* it about this garter belt?"

"Darned if I know, but there's just something about women being clothed—almost—but being mostly naked that just about turns guys' brains around inside their skulls. Aren't you *ever* going to ask me to take off my shorts?"

She tilted her head and moved her eyes around, knowing he watched as she considered. Then she confided, leaning close as if to impart a hushed opinion, "I don't know what's trying to escape, but it looks dangerous. Maybe you'd better keep them on."

He laughed. "Don't be such a coward. It's friendly. You went swimming with it and nothing happened. I think you should get acquainted."

She bit her reddened lower lip as she admitted, "I hesitate to inquire how it shakes hands?"

"Honey, you have me so pitched that I need to put the condom on now. Do you want me to stay here and be discreet or go over there and put it on?"

She was decisive. "I'll do it."

The jolt that went through him at the very idea of her touching him was stunning. He went rigid in the rest of his body, too. He replied gravely, "Not this time."

She was logical. "I should learn to do it. Now's a good time to start."

"Not yet." He was very sure. "I might not last, and you'd have to sit around, sighing and smoking dirty, old

cigarette butts or maybe only cigar stubs until it got re-
fueled.''

He'd mentioned an intensely interesting subject she
hadn't considered. "You can't just...do it continu-
ously?''

"You can!" He wasn't sure he wasn't appalled by the
idea.

She shrugged. "I don't know."

"Well, I do need to put on the condom."

She promised, "I'll watch.''

With a mind-searching frown, he hesitated thoughtfully. "I don't recall ever having had anyone...
watch.''

"You're nervous, too?'' She was charmed.

"I believe so.''

"Aw, Lemon, don't be. It'll be okay.''

She was serious. He wasn't above taking advantage
of her soothing his jitters. He was so pitched that his
hands shook. She could believe that was caused by
nerves, but he was stressed because he needed her.

So she watched. She sat up and folded her hands on
her naked lap as he peeled his shorts to his knees. He
tore away the foil and began to roll the condom on his
rigid sex. It was fascinating, and she kept reaching over
and trying to help, and she about had him on his ear.

She said, "You really do that very well. Have you had
a good deal of practice?''

He wiped his hands on his half-mast shorts and
looked into her big eyes. "This is my first time with
you.''

"Well, I do realize that, but have you had a whole
slew of other women?''

"Not that I recall.''

"Your brain's fuzzed by sexual heat." She guessed that.

"Mor'n likely." He removed his shorts from his knees and pitched them aside. He took her into his arms and kissed her a killer kiss. This one was different. He was no longer coaxing, he was serious. He told her, "Love me."

But with the words he'd said, he became very serious. So serious that his eye wrinkles were white and the back of his throat clacked. With his hands, he coaxed her against him and moved his chest along her so that her sweet breasts rubbed his hairy chest.

To her that was the most erotic experience she'd ever encountered. Her sensitive nipples swooned as they recognized the countering of the male body, and she was thrilled. She swallowed noisily and breathed through her mouth rather stridently.

That's when he knew he had her. He was almost overmanned by the long foreplay of getting her accustomed to him. His body was frantic. He was so embarrassed by his sex acting so eager that he crowded against her for her body to prevent it from bouncing around, and he kissed her.

He slowly tilted her back so that she lay in his arms, and his holding her was all that kept her hovering over the strange clothes-bed laid on the hay. She allowed his easing her on down.

He stretched out beside her, and he was so busy that he didn't talk at all, but he made relishing sounds that were hungry.

His hands already knew her and they went back to his new territory. He asked her in a careful way, "Why are you so wet?"

She gasped in shock that he would mention something so intimate.

By then he was saying, "How lovely you are." His voice was husky, and he panted. He asked her, "Do you like me to do this?"

She moved in a countering manner to make his rubbing more intimate, and her eyes closed as she slowly sucked in air.

He was so hyper by then that his damp hair trembled with his heartbeats. His eyes were fires as he questioned, "How about that?"

She slithered.

"Or this?"

And she moaned.

He settled into long, really serious kissing, and she became maulable and faint. She pawed at him, not aware how she was clawing at his back and pulling at him so that she could get her body under his.

He gave her deep kisses. Then he lowered himself slowly, slowly into the cradle of her love.

He was being so careful that she reached to help place him. She was so determined that inadvertently she was rather rough in pulling him to her.

Outside of flinching a bit, he only said, "You animal."

That made her laugh so that she was relaxed when he encountered her barrier and worked on through. She became wide-eyed and serious and very still.

He leaned on his elbows and waited for her mental adjustment to his invasion of her. Sweating, panting, he kissed in soft caresses along her cheek. He trembled terribly. His serious breathing was very agitated and intense.

He knew that no woman ever realizes the drain on a man who, for the first time, is having sex with a timid and untrained woman. The man is always thought of as doing it for enjoyment. The woman never considers the thankless chore of his horrific restraint.

When he knew her better, he'd explain it all to her.

His shivering was violent and drops of hot sweat dripped from him. He was at his limit. He moved a little, and her eyes got bigger. He tarried a bit; then he had no choice. He moved. He gasped and was fleetingly disappointed with his lack of control, but he'd consider that later.

He made love to her as a man chooses. He went ahead. He knew she was still adjusting, but his limit was past. He pumped and shuddered and gasped and climaxed in a world-class orgasm that addled his mind and just about sundered his body, but it took care of his need.

He collapsed on her, but remembered to brace his forearms enough so that he didn't crush her slender, fragile body. With the several active brain cells still working, he was careful of her. His mind was swamped with his debilitating release, and he almost passed out.

He hadn't been so affected since the second time. The first had been so technical that his mind had really only been an observer. This time had been a flame-out.

It scared him a little. A man really wants to be in control. Could she do this to him? Could he become— addicted to her? Her slave? He'd heard of men in that bind. Look what had happened to John Brown with Lucilla.

Still dripping sweat, Lemon wobbled as he laboriously lifted himself up onto trembling elbows and looked on this lure, this lorelei.

She was very alert, twitchy, her tongue darted out and moistened her swollen red lips. Her eyes were enormous. She was fidgety and restless. She was still triggered.

He groaned and heaved himself off to her side to collapse. This was what they meant when they said a man's work was never done. He put a hand to his forehead and sighed at the burden.

She lifted up and hovered over him like a vampire ready to suck the rest of him dry. She said in some alarm, "Are you all right?"

Outside a groan, he managed one word. "Beached."

It was a silent while before he heaved up enough to remove the condom and put it in his pants pocket to dispose of it later.

Watching with alert interest, Renata leaned back on her elbows, a stunning picture of feminine beauty. Her breasts were reddened from his attentions and his abrasively hairy chest. Her lips were puffed and red. Her attention was riveted on him with great curiosity. She said, "I can't believe it could become soft and almost relax. It's exhausted."

He groaned, "Don't make me laugh, I haven't the energy."

There was a slight silence.

He was wondering what she would do and what she would say next. His conscience niggled that he'd been her first and he should be tender with her. But what if she was another Lucilla and wanted to put her efforts into liquidating his bank account? His mind spun on.

She was still astounded by his performance. "It completely wrecked you."

"Yeah."

"You're really beached. It was the perfect word for you to choose. It's quite visual."

His eyes closed. He made an agreeing sound, but didn't move.

"You're totally limp."

He flinched in automatic reflex as she gently touched him. "It takes a lot out of a guy."

She laughed a bubble of humor.

He had to smile a little bit, and could. But he wondered if she was new to all the old jokes, too? It would be unique to hear laughter from a woman, instead of being topped with another old chestnut.

She asked, "How long before you can do it again? I realize right now isn't the time, but I am interested in whatever is the female counterpart to whatever happened to you. I'm about to climb the wall."

"I can give you relief now."

She looked down him dubiously. "It'll go back in?"

He was hard put not to guffaw. However, in his inert state, he did manage to keep it to a faint smile, but his white crinkles disappeared. "I can massage you nicely, and you'll love it."

"I . . . don't think so. I'll wait."

He opened one eye to monitor her reaction. "I'll feel like a rabbit being eyed by a hawk."

She considered quite charmingly. She looked out over the fragile land that showed no promise of improving, and she said, "I'll be a . . . subtle hawk."

And he laughed. Impossibly, he rolled up and took her against him and hugged her. He growled low and amused, "You siren."

She frowned, considering. "I'm shrill?"

"You're seductive."

She brightened. "You're ready again?"

"Not yet."

"How long?" She tilted her head seriously intent.

He sighed, long-suffering, and complained, "A bloodsucker. A voracious woman. A buzzard."

She scoffed. "I'm all that?"

"My tender sex is terrified."

"I should reassure it?"

His eyes slitted, and he smiled wickedly. "You could try."

She pushed gently on his chest until he lay flat again. She leaned over and lay her sweet, pinkened cheek against him as she said softly, "Don't be scared, I won't hurt you."

He became very alert. He held his breath and watched avidly.

She looked up his body into his eyes and smiled just a little; then she turned her face and kissed him gently.

He sucked in air and said, "I believe a miracle is happening."

And she laughed.

She reached up, and her fingers played in the hair on his chest. Her hand followed the swirls of the patterns and she smoothed them into order. She was fascinated by the pattern around his navel.

In turn, she fascinated him. And his body loved her attentions. He smiled in rueful delight as his sex responded to her interest. He was susceptible to her. He said, "It just don't get no better'n this."

She lifted her mouth from her coaxing and looked at him with a grin. "You're lazy and like attention."

"Yes'm, I surely do."

She scoffed. "You're easy."

"I believe I could become a slave to you." He was mostly serious and watched her.

"I'd be annoyed by any man who hung onto my skirts."

"What would he hang on if you were in shorts or jeans?"

She smiled and shrugged. But that called his attention to her body. Hell, her body had had his attention all along.

And she was now concentrated on exploring his. It was stimulating to say the least. Her curiosity was erotic. She was just fortunate that he'd gone ahead that first time. He could probably be slower this time. Maybe. "Whooeee!" he gasped and leaned his head back in a flood of ecstatic arousal. "How do you expect me to survive this day?"

"Should I stop?" She was serious. "I was really curious. Am I being too bold?"

"No. Don't stop, and you can be as curious as you want. Go on. Touch me there again. Yeah. I like that. But I like it when you kiss me, too. You haven't kissed me yet."

"I did so."

"That was the first time. This is a whole new ball game."

And she replied, "Yes."

She slowly dragged her bare, bumpy body up his hairy one, and he was so riveted by the sensation that he didn't help her at all. She finally reached his mouth and found him hungry and much stronger than he'd appeared.

She found he wasn't depleted after all. He found a condom in his wallet, and she'd been playing with fire. But the burning was exquisitely thrilling, the coupling was perfect, and the climax was beyond everything she had anticipated.

She was glad she'd waited for Lemon.

They lay, depleted and contented. She made sweet sounds that filled his soul. His soul had never before shown interest in a woman. It absorbed her little sounds as if it had been parched for such murmurs from Renata.

Nine

Lemon and Renata had had no lunch. He gave her water from the hidden well. And he shared some cookies in a covered pot on a shelf in the shack.

On that elevated terrain in a three-sided shed, they lolled on the skimpily padded hay next to the convertible. Having shared their bodies in the most intimate manner, they exchanged ideas as they became acquainted.

They listened to each others' opinions and sometimes agreed. They recounted and shared hilarious times. Hers were scant. And he considered that her life had been very limited.

He asked, "How did you learn bridge?"

"When my great-aunt was still living, I was drafted to fill in for anyone absent in her bridge club. They felt I could manage when I passed the age of ten. They were very stern with me. There is nothing more shriveling than the stern, dismissive glance of a wrinkled old lady. They were all 'ladies.' "

He nodded as a sharing only child raised in a sea of adults. "I learned poker first. The players' attitudes are similar."

"Cutthroat." She said that in an accepting way.

"I should hope to tell you." He agreed and smiled. "My teachers were dirty old men. Physically dirty, mentally reasonably normal. Anyone who goes out and takes care of beeves isn't working with a full deck."

"Bridge."

"I'm not sure 'working with a full deck' was bridge. It could have been poker. Or hearts. There were great conversations, storytelling. It was really interesting to hear the old-timers discuss past things, problems and how they were solved. I learned a lot from them.

"And being an only child, I played hearts a whole lot. And solitaire. Time-passing things when I needed to be around for some reason and couldn't ride out with the men."

She made sounds of understanding. Then she told him, "I was never given time alone, except when I was reading in the library. I daydreamed over opened books."

"What'd you dream about?" he asked nicely.

She looked at him with those large eyes and replied, "You."

That one word was an aphrodisiac.

By then they'd used up his two condoms, and they had to take the backup one from her purple garter belt. He found removing it from that hidden pocket was incredibly erotic.

With their third encounter, she winced a tad with his entry, but she held him close so he wasn't aware. They spent a long, leisurely time experimenting, laughing, teasing and becoming very lazily sexual. It was love of another kind.

They didn't return to the house until after five. They managed to sneak up one of the back stairwells and go to their rooms to bathe and change. Renata covered the whisker burns on her face with cream and then lightly powdered the surface quite carefully.

Her eyes looked back at her and she was stimulated and amused. She gave herself a wink, and then wondered why she'd chosen that communication with her mirrored self.

The errant couple met in the upper hallway and smiled at each other for some time. It would be hopeless for them to participate in the general scheme of things. It would take a while for them to realize they were a part of the real world.

They appeared at a buffet supper on the lawn. The staff had used that ploy in order to clear the bridge tables from the ballroom for the evening's dance.

The supper was succulent, eye-catching finger food. The lovers' quietness was not particularly noticed because the games had been intense and fought to the wall. The players were full of themselves and still arguing about hands played that morning and mentioning what their partners *should* have done.

Probably the only ones who noticed the hooky players were John, of course, Lucilla and the barn cat.

When a decent amount of time had elapsed, the errant pair drifted off upstairs to get some sleep. But after Renata was settled into her bed, she heard a key turn quietly in her lock. She sat up in some indignantly cautious surprise, with her hand reaching for the house phone.

Lemon came through her door, closed and locked it again before he came to her bed. He very naturally lifted the sheet and light blanket so that he could slide into her bed beside her. He did that, pulled her over to him and settled her nicely. He was then still and silent.

She inquired, "What are you doing in here?"

He said, "Shhh."

She was amused. She smiled at the ceiling and was aware she was very comfortable. She wondered if she could handle another romp? She was a little tender.

To the soft, filtered music from the ballroom, she went to sleep, waiting.

Some time in the night the by-then-separated lovers met in the middle of the bed and were delighted.

It just so happened he had condoms—with an *S*—in his pajama pocket. And he used one.

The bed was better than the contrived bed on the hay.

The next day the cook and barn cat continued to substitute for the vapid pair who wandered around, holding hands, talking about nothing and smiling all the while.

As his fingers rubbed in his beard, John said to Lemon, "We need to talk. Word of your financial demise is spreading across TEXAS...and will soon be known in other states and foreign countries."

Lemon smiled kindly and clarified responsibility. "Your job."

John was calm and logical. "We need to discuss a strategy."

"You'll figure it out."

John was disgusted. Lemon had never been vague. He was an organizer who kept every string locked in his iron grasp. Then John's brain slowly cleared as he looked at his friend. Lemon really was zonked by that Renata Gunther. For the first time in Lemon's life, someone else came before his business!

Lemon had always been considerate of people. His business sense demanded that his people all be focused, cared for and contented, but with enough stress to be excited. He didn't want his people to become too concentrated or too limited. They had to have wider life experiences.

Just the fact that the cook was a tournament bridge player was a clue to that. And the fact that Lemon had talked Margot into coming last New Year's Eve so that she could trap John Brown was another. Lemon cared about people.

Standing in his house office, John considered his employer. Lemon was acting out of character.

Was Lemon grilling John on what was happening all over the world? No. Was Lemon checking the phone-call list? No. Was he sifting through John's notes on his desk? No. Lemon was looking out the window, relaxed, vague, his hands in his pockets. The dog, Hunter, was biting at his paw, bored out of his gourd.

John began his lecture, "Lemon—"

Lemon smiled at his earnest financial adviser and clapped John's shoulder with one big hand. "Take care of it, please." And Lemon wandered off, looking for Renata.

Hunter *whuffed* once and pinned John with his stare. John opened the window and pushed aside the screen. Hunter went outside.

John sought Margot and asked, "Is this Renata Gunther right for Lemon?"

And without hesitating, Margot said a positive "Yes."

He took a step or two before he inquired carefully, "Have you heard the rumor about Lemon's finances?"

Her face bland with disinterest, she replied, "Right away. Just about as soon as he used that ruse to avoid being Lucilla's *next* victim."

"Now, Margot, Lucilla isn't vindictive."

Margot gave him a startled, unbelieving look.

He chided gently, "Jealousy is beneath a woman like you."

She puffed a *"Pah!"* of disbelief.

He smothered his smile and took another step before he told Margot, "When Lucilla asked for the check to withdraw her investment in L.C. Partners, L.P., Lucilla said people should know that a fine man like Lemon might need some friendly support."

Margot closed her eyes down to slits and thinned her lips.

With gentle determination, John took her resisting body into his arms as he said, "There is no mystery to you, Margot, you are arrow straight, aboveboard and honest as the day is long."

She countered sassily and argumentatively, "I'm seductive and gorgeous."

He pushed his lower lip up and looked at nothing as he considered her reply. "Yeah. That about covers it."

She pushed. "I'm also brilliant, kind and loving."

"You are brilliant. I need to see the kind and loving part a little more."

"You want me to be *kind* to that witch?"

In celebration and congratulation, he exclaimed, "You used the *W!*"

She tilted her nose. "I'm a lady."

"Well, you are female, I made sure of that."

Margot was serious. She lay in John's arms, and her fingers touched his bearded cheek to get his earnest attention. "John, Lemon is going to break Renata's heart. Look how he's stolen all of her time this weekend. And he's given her all of his attention. Have you ever seen Lemon have the time for a woman?"

John remembered the long time Lemon had used on the Saturday before New Year's when he'd stood on Margot's porch and talked her into coming to his house for New Year's Eve... and wearing that sinful, red spangled dress.

And John remembered that Lemon had been around and available the entire weekend to be sure that Margot was cared for. When Lemon wanted to, he had the time to patch things or to change things or to share things.

But Margot was continuing. "Lemon's allowing Renata to believe she can have his attention. Would you ever believe Lemon would give up a bridge tournament for a woman?"

John said honestly, "Lemon doesn't much care for bridge."

Margot said, "Bosh." She was disturbed and earnest. She said, "His behavior with Renata is misleading. He is behaving like a normal person."

John considered thoughtfully and responded, "Normally, he's reasonably normal."

Margot shook an impatient head. "This is courting behavior. He was with her all evening on Friday, all day yesterday, and he's giving today to her. She is mesmerized."

"Yeah." John smiled mushily and added, "Like you were with me."

"I don't need you to be at my elbow all day. Renata will need a man who pays attention to her. Lemon will seem like an attentive lover. He isn't."

"He is interested in her. He's been paying attention."

"That's courting. He wants her in his bed, and in order to accomplish that, he is attentive. When he's used to using her, he will become interested in something else. He will be distracted. Men are that way."

"Well, I think it would be difficult for a man to stand at a woman's elbow, all the time, or to kneel at her feet."

"Doing such a thing would be a nuisance, and you know it."

John hugged Margot close, as he told her, "I'd be glad to be at your elbow and on my knees if you're giving me a lecture on neglect?"

"No." Margot allowed John to hold her as she lay her cheek on his collarbone. "If you hung around all the time, I'd probably tear my hair."

He agreed, but expanded on it. "While you're clever and beautiful and—"

Impatiently, she corrected, "'Straight arrow, aboveboard and honest—'"

He added, "Seductive and beautiful and brilliant?"

She threw in, "Kind and loving—"

"I don't remember kind and loving. Am I missing something?"

Margot snarled, "You beast!"

John laughed.

She stiff-armed him and enunciated, "Lemon is like all men. They chase and court and win a woman with all their attention. And having won her, they put her aside and go back to what interests them."

John was listening, for he said, "I've neglected you lately."

"I'm not talking about us. I'm talking about a woman who was so isolated from reality that she will expect too much of Lemon. She is hungry for companionship. Have you seen her? Her eyes shine. She smiles for no reason. She is wallowing in his attention."

John said, "He seems pretty zonked. I believe he's in love with her."

But Margot was deadly serious. "He will have no time for her. You know that. She could be devastated. She will think his neglect is temporary. That thinking could last for years and years before she understands he never planned to live any other way but his own way. And for him, it's normal. He could break her heart."

"Well, I must admit their attraction happened pretty fast. He—"

"You must tell Lemon to back off from her until she can realize exactly what sort of life she will have with him."

"Now, Margot, they just met Friday night. You're seeing ghosts."

"They've almost constantly been together since then. This may be a quirk for Lemon, but for a woman like Renata, this is a very serious happening."

John said what Margot wanted to hear. He promised, "I'll speak to Lemon. But Renata isn't you, nor is she a person who needs the presence of another in order to be contented or to feel loved. She is different. However, I will speak to Lemon."

She said a formal, "Thank you. It is necessary. You aren't doing this for me. You're doing it for Renata. Better that she knows now, than to pine and suffer for years and years."

"My parents love one another and live side by side. But my dad is retired from the navy."

"You know how my parents are, but not all married couples can be friends and lovers. It's a serious mistake to believe it."

"Are you suggesting we start living together to see how we rub together?"

She sighed as she looked off to the side and lifted her eyebrows. "That again."

"Living together?"

"Rubbing."

He smiled and coughed a couple of chuffs. "I'm not used to you enough to survive such salacious conversations."

"You'll learn. As soon as we're married, you'll be at the office all the time, and I'll sit home with the kids."

He counted it out. "With your family, your friends, your clubs, your new car—"

"What new car?"

"The one I'm going to get you. That way, if you have wheels, you'll let me go to the office and work so I can feed the kids."

"You're very calculating."

"I'm a business major."

The bridge players played hell-bent all day Sunday. The cook-substitute player was critical and thoughtful of the food served, but she said nothing. Everyone else exclaimed over the food. They did that when they weren't talking about bridge, the last hand, about a game that day or about one played fifteen years ago.

After lunch, the guests went outside to stretch their legs as the house staff freshened the ballroom, realigned the tables and chairs and put fresh cards, score pads and pencils on the tables.

Lemon noted that Lucilla was being charming to Pots's friend Silas. Lemon watched Silas and noted that he was a man who could handle knowing Lucilla.

And Pots? An amused Pots was following along after a rather prissy-acting Beatrice. It was she who had caught Lemon's eye that first day. Was it only the day before yesterday? It seemed like weeks, so much had happened.

What had happened? Renata. He had to be sure of her before she learned the rumors of his financial worries were not true. He smiled down at her head as he thought of sleeping in her bed the night before. How had he found her?

He said, "Come out and see my pinto."

"Okay, but I have seen him. He looks like a challenge."

"He is." Lemon agreed.

"Have you decided to let me ride him?"

"No."

"I can look but not touch?" Her eyes were teasing and her cheeks were pink.

"You look at me thataway and everybody will know you cotton to me."

"No." She looked delightfully innocent, glancing aside and pretending she didn't have all of his attention. She had the audacity to add, "I'm only being courteous."

"Is that what you call what we've been doing?" He was shocked.

She laughed, but she went scarlet. He loved it that she did, that she was new for him. He felt new. He was having trouble keeping his hands from her body, from touching her cheek or hand. He was sundered by her.

Was she? He looked at her and thought she was the most beautiful woman in all of the universe. He said to her in a low, intimate voice, "Tonight, we'll go up on the top of the house and you can show me which star is the sun for your planet."

She told him snippily, "It's the one beaming down on this one."

"You're really human?"

She pretended shock. "You haven't noticed?"

"Well, I did hear you belch this noon at—"

"I did not, either!" But she laughed and swatted his shoulder in a nothing blow. She was flirting.

He captured her hand and kissed it. Everyone saw him do that. Well, almost everyone, and like the news of his financial problems, the news spread that Lemon Covington was interested in that Gunther woman—the Gunther Orphan—the reclusive great-grandniece of Minerva Gunther. It depended on the age of the observer as to how she was classified. And it was added that she also had some means.

There were those who asked "Who?" because she hadn't been circulated very much as she was maturing. And she just hadn't been around since then, either.

Means? That had perked up one man's ears. He remembered hearing that she had a tidy little fortune. He looked at who they were discussing and was surprised. He left the group that was talking about her and pretended to wander around, but he really was obvious in calling Renata's attention to himself.

He'd never seen her before then, and she was quite attractive. That was a surprise. Most women who had means were either married, too old, too young or ugly.

He smiled kindly and said, "I'm Charlotte Waggoner's grandson, Theo Waggoner? I believe you played bridge with her. I recall her speaking of you. Aren't you playing today?"

Lemon replied pleasantly, "I've been teaching her to skinny-dip."

While Theo only blinked once in shock, his libido was stimulated by the flash of imagining Renata naked in a pool. Renata might not be as difficult to snare as he'd thought.

But she was shocked pale. She gasped.

Lemon went on nicely, "In the pond. The scruffy yella dog, Hunter, and I stand guard so no one peeks or insists on swimming with her."

Theo considered that Lemon was about as scruffy as the yellow dog. And Lemon's fortunes were failing. Theo's were secure. And he'd gotten his money out of Lemon's faltering Limited Partners. He moved with confidence and, ignoring Lemon, crowding him aside as, in a mannerly way, he asked Renata pleasantly, "Playing this afternoon?"

Lemon replied, "With me." He wasn't hostile or belligerent. He was kind in discarding the intruder.

Renata was fascinated. She'd spent her life as a brown wren. And here she was dressed in a silk dress that was a subtly splashed combination of greens. Her hair was up in the new way with a green band and the tortoise pins. In her ears were long, dangling pearls.

And there, before her, were two men who were figuratively arching their backs, with their nostrils flared and making hostile noises in a courteous way. Over her! Over Renata Gunther. Such only happened in books!

It was heady.

Even before it sounded, Lemon glanced at his watch and mentioned, "There's the gong." And it sounded. Lemon smiled.

Theo turned to Renata and said, "You played the grand slam with the first hand. Why not come partner me? I could use your expertise."

"Sorry." Lemon said that and smiled at Theo in a one-upmanship manner. He took Renata's hand and put it on his arm. Never taking his eyes from the intruder, Lemon bowed his head once to Theo. He moved Renata so that it was his body between her and Theo.

Theo wasn't easily put off. He moved and crossed over in back of them to be beside Renata. He said, "Do come partner me." And he boldly took her other arm.

She smiled up at Theo and replied, "Excuse us." Then she turned her head to watch her steps as she walked along beside Lemon.

Lemon was so pleased. He was asinine enough that he glanced smugly back at Theo, but That One was watching down Renata's backside.

Flame burst inside Lemon. Jealousy. A great motivator for a man to seal up a woman, one way or the other if not actually.

He looked forward to be sure the way was clear, then he looked back again. Theo was still standing there, watching after Renata. It ticked Lemon off.

As they walked past John, Lemon said, "Tell Theo Waggoner that his mother wants him."

John replied pragmatically, "I believe his mother is deceased."

Lemon said over his shoulder, "Send Theo to see her."

They walked four paces in silence before the giggles hit Renata. She raised her glance to Lemon's and her humor was spilling from them. "That was wicked."

"No." Lemon was sure.

"Of course, it was. You're a better host than that."

"If I was a better host—" he enunciated clearly "—I'd be playing bridge."

"You played." She turned her head in a very smooth manner as she looked around, allowing him to guide her along.

He was also looking around. He explained, "I played . . . with you."

"I mean bridge," she elaborated.

"I meant that first. When we weren't playing bridge, we played together."

"I swam alone."

He looked around again and corrected her, "At first."

"Are you ruining my reputation?"

"Probably."

"How shocking." She said that with deliberately tightened lips, but her cheeks were hot and her eyes were filled with humor.

And Lemon laughed. He said, "Do you have riding clothes here? Jeans?"

"Yes. Am I going to ride the pinto?"

"No. Sorry. I have to. Nobody will work him. He gets nasty and feels he can run his own life and schedule it as he chooses. It's always up to me to do something about him."

"I understand Lucilla can handle the pinto."

Lemon nodded as he agreed, "Brilliantly."

"Why don't you give him to her?" It was so logical.

Lemon's voice went up seven octaves as he asked, "Give *her* the *pinto?* You're crazy!"

"It's logical. She can handle him, and he'll do as she says. Give her the horse."

Lemon groused, "She'll think I'm trying for her."

Rather airily, with wonderful confidence, she soothed him. "I'll straighten her out on that."

"So you think I'm trying for you?"

She corrected, "No. Not anymore."

He was indignant. "Oh, yes, I am."

She shrugged her shoulders in a lovely way, as she told him, "You've got me."

His voice was reedy, "Rennie . . ."

"Rennie?"

"That's what I call you to myself."

"I like it."

Very seriously, he told her, "I like you."

"I believe that's very fortunate." She tilted her head back and looked up at him. Then she explained, "Because I'm going to get you."

In a hoarse whisper, he informed her in a complaining manner, "You've already had me too many times. It fell off this morning in the shower."

And she laughed. She giggled and then put back her head and just laughed. She had a wonderful laugh.

He licked at his own smile and finally chided, "It isn't funny."

"Maybe we can glue it back on."

He brightened and suggested urgently, "Let's go try."

"What have I said!"

"That you're a compassionate woman and you want to help me survive."

She was a little indignant. "Who is going to help me?"

"I'll put you on my list. Come up to my room. We used yours last night, this time we use mine."

She was a stickler. "We're going to exercise the pinto."

He looked at her distastefully. "You're really a pain." Then he brightened. "Want to know where? Come upstairs to my room, and I'll show you."

"I need to change into jeans so we can ride."

Smokily, he corrected, "We can ride without the jeans."

She told him, "Only bare *Playboy* models ride bareback."

He was shocked. "How do you know that?"

"I saw a tape."

"Why, Miss Gunther, you are a surprise!"

She shrugged her shoulders. "Apparently not. You have not even once exclaimed or protested or anything in all this time."

He leaned over and told her earnestly, "I was too shocked to speak."

And she laughed.

They did change their clothing and then went down to the corral. Lemon wore a gun belt and in the holster was a real gun. Renata looked at it seriously. "You need the gun?"

"Better to not need it and have it, than to need it and not. We wear guns. Along with creature surprises or animals needing help, this is a mean time, with a lot of people moving around without wanting to be seen."

"That sounds like olden times. Not this time of living. How can it be so violent? What's happening to this country?"

"There're too many people. There are too many of those who are greedy. They don't live by the rules. They don't study and strive. They want it easy."

She was very sobered. "Yes. It's that way in the cities. Many people have guns in their houses and in their cars. People are killed. I thought it would be different—out here—out here in the wide, open spaces."

"Living, dealing with problems, striving, competing is the same anywhere. Let's go exercise the horses. It's another thing that has to be done."

So she went along silently. The real world was scary. Who would think that sparse, peaceful countryside could hold danger for people from other people?

They went out of the house, walking quietly, and she only then noted how often Lemon looked around. How constantly he was alert to the area. His head turned and his eyes moved over the land, missing nothing.

She remembered when they'd gone into the hills to the ancestors' place, he'd been very careful.

There was more to living than she'd ever known in her isolated ivory tower of poetry and painting.

And she wondered if she was woman enough to take up such a different life than the one she'd known.

Ten

Having called on the house phone for the horses to be ready, the two lovers walked out to the stable. The air was wonderful TEXAS summer hotness, and the breeze was dry and perfect.

The mare for Renata to ride was ready, and Peanuts, the great lug of a stableman, said to her in his most mannerly way, "Go ahead and get out of the way. The pinto is a little impatient."

Renata was a good rider. As a child, it had been a way of not playing bridge with her great-aunt. Renata mounted, watched by the sober-faced stable hands who were, in turn, watched by a serious Lemon.

Renata took the mare out of the yard and went on beyond.

Two men brought out the pinto and, standing by

Hunter, Lemon watched sourly. He groused, "Why the hell can't you guys exercise that damned horse?"

Peanuts was astonished. "And get hurt? We're delicate. *We* know better than to try to get on that dumb animal. He's a mean horse."

The stable hands all backed away as, alone, Lemon mounted the horse.

With Hunter running alongside, Lemon rode the damned pinto. He went the opposite way of the track taken by Renata. The pinto had to run to help him get rid of excess energy. When he simply ran, it was a glorious sharing between horse and rider. And Lemon again loved the horse. It was exhilarating. The horse was a runner.

The pinto and his rider met Renata and her horse. Unfortunately, the mare had just come into season. The pinto wanted to mount the mare, and Lemon fought his horse as Renata and her mare watched in bafflement. Then Lemon called to Renata to get off her horse.

The pinto was determined.

Hunter was a big dog, and he went to stand between the pinto and Renata's mare. His bark was serious, and he got Renata the time to dismount.

Then the big dog advanced threateningly on the pinto, distracting him enough that Lemon had the time to get off the damned horse. No one could have removed the pinto's saddle or, by then, the mare's. Lemon just stood there and gave up. Then he strolled over to the shocked-eyed Renata.

"I'm sorry," Lemon began.

And Renata said, "Wow!"

Lemon laughed and hugged his woman.

Having heard the hubbub, the hands came racing their horses to help. But they found the aggressive horse temporarily quiet, and the two humans walking back.

One of the men reset the pinto's saddle while another stripped the frisky mare. The men gave a gelded horse to Renata and helped her mount. With seeming mildness, Lemon said to Peanuts, "You could have mentioned the mare was in season."

And Peanuts, with urgent softness, said approximately, "Honest to God, Lemon, I didn't know the lady was riding with you. I thought she was going by herself. The mare must have just come into it. Of all the things I'd do to annoy you, I'd never harm a lady."

Lemon already knew that.

The mare was taken back to the stable. Renata had to mention, "How typical to punish the mare, when the pinto was to blame."

Lemon slid his wicked eyes over to her and explained, "This way, her colt will be the pinto's."

While Lemon rode the surfeited pinto, Renata's steed was gelded and easy to ride. By then, so was the pinto... for a while.

Lemon said to his lovely companion, "I'm really ticked you were put in danger, but I have to sympathize with the pinto. I know just how he felt... when I look at you."

"You have more élan."

And Lemon put back his head and laughed. When he could, he said, "I hope you never know how close I come to acting just like that stud."

She arched one eyebrow as she looked over at him and said, "Yes."

The two rode for a long way. They talked and laughed. Their horses were interested in looking around and communicating in a manner of snorts and blowing chuffs and head turnings. Hunter flicked an ear to the horses' communication and gave an occasional *wuff* in comment.

Lemon said to Renata, "You ride well."

"Thank you." Renata smiled and looked over at him. "I learned to ride in order to avoid at least some sessions of bridge."

"You're a great bridge player. The only trouble is you squirm your bottom around on your chair and lick your lips and bite your lower lip and mess up your hair and drive me wild."

"Playing bridge turns you on?"

"You squirming around thataway does it."

Quite seriously, she said again, "It meant a great deal to me that you trusted me to play the grand-slam bid, and you didn't interfere at all. It was heady."

How could he ever tell her that he hadn't cared whether she'd won the game or not? "I've already told you that you're a great bridge player." He looked over at her. "You ride well, too."

She smiled at him; then she lifted her face to the sky and breathed deeply. "It's wonderful to share an adventure with a horse. To be out, away from everything. The park's rules were limiting. Galloping was frowned on. We could trot on occasion. But a full-out run was forbidden. I thought it must be very dull for those horses. No adventure."

Lemon could agree. "Yeah."

She commented, "You are leading me deliberately to a particular place. Where are we going?"

He wasn't at all surprised that she'd figured it out. "I have to check on a line cabin and a cattle-watering place. We'll be putting a herd into this area soon. We've allowed this part to lie fallow. The project is under the strict supervision of the farm bureau.

"Several years ago, we had the first of the Yankee sludge shipped in. A whole trainload. It was then mixed with some of this spent soil and good grass seed. By truck, it was distributed onto the land."

He pointed with his chin toward the ridge. "You'll see it soon. This is an experiment. While animal droppings have been used as fertilizer all along, and are still, in the Far East human waste was used and is used. But that isn't treated and diseases run wild. After the cholera epidemics, here and in Europe, human waste was not used as fertilizer."

In an aside, he explained, "The fact that people eat meat is a contributing factor in treating the sludge so that it will be safe.

"As everybody knows, our waste is a mind-boggling problem in the cities. It pollutes rivers and even the oceans, but if we can treat it so that it can be used, it's good land fertilizer."

He said it again. "It's an experiment. Around and about, there are several places trying this out. It will be used only for cattle grazing in all the experiments. Some places are putting the sludge on the top of the ground without mixing it with soil. We chose to have it mixed and paid the difference.

"If it works, and there are no repercussions, farmers and cattlemen could solve all the cities' problems. So far we're not growing anything for the market in the sludge, we're just allowing cattle to graze and add their own contributions."

They had reached the top of a rise. Hunter was already there, looking around and then looking back to the people. Beyond was a section that looked like a sea of subtle greenery. They sat their horses, noting the limit of the greenery.

She asked, "Are there sprays to keep it moist?"

"No. That's part of the experiment. The kinds of grasses planted here are native to this arid area. The native grasses have been overgrazed. The thinness of the hoof-torn soil around the surviving plants allowed the seldom rains to erode the root systems."

She was impressed. "Look at the difference!"

"This new section was probably how it looked three hundred years ago, when my people first came out this way. Man greedily ruins things without thinking ahead or having any plans. Like the terrible mutilation of the West by the gold seekers. Those ravaged lands may never heal.

"We always thought the land wouldn't be used up, but it is already, all over the world. We are too many people now. We're on the very brink of ruining this world. It would be a miracle if we can use our pollution to improve what's left. Everything should rot so that it can be absorbed and reused."

Looking around, she said almost absently, "Skulls take the longest."

With her words, he saw her as a fragile miracle who was limited in time. The pang that went through him was startling. Did he really love her? This soon? That much?

The two humans, who so briefly marked their passage in this time, got off their horses and walked a way into the vigorous grass, slowly leading the horses. The horses weren't hungry, but they nipped a little and chewed as they looked around.

Lemon squatted down and pulled a handful, testing the root system, then put it back and tamped the roots down into the accepting soil with his booted foot. "I can't believe it. It is a miracle. And this weather has helped. I wonder if it will survive the really bad times."

"Well, some years ago they thought the Edwards aquifer was doomed. Then in 1992 the rains revived it to overflowing the underground limestone. The grass had to've been growing before then."

He smiled at her for that comment and agreed. "Yeah."

"Quite some time ago, near the treatment plant, my aunt took up the offer to clear away free sludge for gardens. I was about nine or ten. They said we were to use it only on grass or flowers, not to use it in a vegetable garden. We got several buckets full. To my aunt's great surprise, we grew marijuana! The seeds were already in the soil. My aunt was unknowing and just thought they were hardy weeds, but we looked them up in the identifying flora dictionary that my aunt had, and the plant was marijuana."

"Any strange visitors to your garden?"

"No. My aunt destroyed them all. She burned them in the fireplace."

"Any of the birds act strange?"

She looked at the clouds while she smiled over that, but she replied, "Not that I recall." Then she added, "I'm not an authority on bird behavior."

And he laughed.

The ground was porous and dry, so there was no residue on their boots. They remounted and rode away up the rise. At the top, they paused to look back at the lovely miracle.

She said, "I hope it works. It would be nice if something does."

"Yeah." Then he mentioned, "We still have to check the line shack and the well."

She made no objection, so he indicated the way and they rode along easily.

Their horses were interested. The dog went on ahead, glancing back to see if they were still with him. He ranged around, relishing being out and away from the tameness of the house.

They came to a fence and rode along it. Other horses came to stand at a distance, to watch their passing. The horses called to those ridden and, oddly, the ridden ones only pricked their ears. Then the pinto said something rude to the stallion who was standing free.

The free stallion bobbed his head, probably in hilarity, and replied with a shrill challenge. So Lemon got to show off his control of a horse in front of Renata. He told her, "Best keep a distance."

The argument between the pinto and Lemon lasted the length of the fence. The pinto danced sideways and tried to buck. Because Renata was within hearing distance, Lemon smothered the words he used in soft tones to communicate with the horse.

The damned loose stallion had to run along on the other side of the fence and say other things, which irritated the hell out of the pinto. By the time they reached the corner of the fenced area, Lemon had worked up a very good sweat, and his temper was edged.

The pinto tried to turn back, but Lemon was adamant they continue in the direction of the cabin.

Finally passing over the rise and out of sight of the free horses, the pinto calmed down enough. The only thing that saved the horse from Lemon's mayhem was that a man's hands wouldn't fit around the horse's throat.

Of course, there was the fact that a dead horse wouldn't carry him back to the house and he'd have to walk it...in boots. Walking any distance in heeled cowboy boots would influence even the most cantankerous cowboy into preserving an impossible horse.

The shack had a windmill and a pond. The holding area for fattening cattle was close to the train spur that ended alongside the chutes. The holding area and chutes were some distance from the shack. It was about rifle distance for shooting anybody who tried for the cattle.

Behind the shack there was the usual three-sided horse shed. At a distance was a privy. Those sat back, downgrade and away from the windmill-supplied pond.

As Lemon began to unsaddle the pinto, he said, "We'll swim. This is almost as good as the creek pond back home."

She considered more mud and controlled her enthusiasm. She began to unsaddle her gelded horse. He was patient.

Lemon lifted the saddle onto a rail as he told her in an aside, "We have to counter the star-burn you suffered from the other night."

Renata smoothed the horse blankets over the same rail to air and dry. She commented, "I hadn't realized that I'd had a star dosage."

"City girl." He shook his head over how limited she was. He lifted her saddle up beside his on the rail.

They took up the reins of the two horses and led them to the mesquite-shaded minicorral in back of the three-sided stable.

She asked, "Is the star dosage acquired out here similar to a cowboy getting a city polish?"

"Yeah. Close." He put some hay down for the horses to nose into, and he saw to it that the water was fresh in their trough.

She had leaned on the top rail to watch him. She said softly, "You polish up real good."

He stood with his hands on his hips, looking at her. He said in a rote, "Thank you, ma'am." Then he said what he wanted to, "Take off your clothes and let me judge how much daylight you might be needing, so's we can counteract that subtle star overdose."

"You're asking me to...disrobe in broad daylight?"

"Yep."

"That seems a rash thing to do out here with no one else around."

He was rather elaborately surprised and, of course, shocked. "You want an *audience?*"

"It just seems risky. You're susceptible to naked women. Even clothed women. You're triggered."

He was logical. "I have protection for you. These aren't the utilitarian type. They're green."

"Green." She assimilated that, trying not to laugh. "I've read that there are polka-dotted ones."

He nodded solemnly. "And there are some with stripes for the big guys to look smaller."

"Hah!" She hooted.

He assured her. "Men try to be subtle."

"Yes? When?"

He replied logically, "When it's necessary."

She scoffed, "Green condoms are not subtle."

"Well, there weren't no other kind. We'll test them and send in a survey of just our opinions as to whether this color was a put-off. We can be anonymous. We need not sign our real names."

She ventured thoughtfully, "I suppose I could close my eyes."

"I'm keeping mine open. You attacked me so fast each and every single time that I never had any chance to see if you're made right. And if you're really from this planet. You know you've made me suspicious?"

"No." She scoffed and waited for his response.

He assured her, "After we were paddling around in the creek pond, I asked you which star shone on your planet."

"I told you it was this sun."

He shook his head in a discarding way. "But you could be trying to fool me into believing you're not magical, that you're an ordinary human."

"Of course. That's the first lesson."

"Ah-*hah!* I knew it! How do you kiss, up yonder where you come from? Show me."

So she reached for him.

They were sweaty and smelling of horse. They didn't notice. They went into the three-sided barn, disrobing each other. Their clothing was a trail showing where they were and where they'd started.

She didn't notice the hay had scant covering. He managed to get his shirt under her back. He grinned at her and said, "You animal."

She took in a gasp of air and replied, "I'm on the bottom."

"Yeah. You got here first and got the best place."

She opened her eyes. "You want to be on the bottom?"

"Why do you think I struggle so hard? I keep fighting you to let me be on the bottom."

She began to wiggle and squirm.

He said, "What's the matter?" He was serious and pulled back, releasing her from his hold. "Are you okay?"

She smiled wickedly. "I'm going to be on top."

He whispered, "Save me. Save me from this voraciously wicked, man-killing woman."

"No one's anywhere around. You're in my power. Lie flat. I've got you where I want you. You came along so innocently. You had no idea we would be so far from help. You're here—alone—with me."

He breathed, "Help. Help." And he spread his hands on his . . . chest.

She laughed so that she had to sit back and just laugh. "You are such a hambone."

"I take a woman's hunger very seriously. Go ahead. Vent your lusts. No. Not there. Lower. A . . . little . . . lower. Yeah. There." Then all the air went out of his lungs at once, and he sucked it back in with all sorts of sounds.

He shivered and twitched and moaned and laughed, and his hot eyes watched her avidly. His hands touched her and squeezed her here and there and rubbed her in some places.

She tried to put the condom on, and they had to find the other one. He told her, "If you'd let me do it, we'd still have a spare."

She closed her eyes down halfway, and her voice was light and wicked. "I have two others."

He pretended to pass out.

She said, "Have you fainted? It isn't the real color. The condom is that green. Under it you're just the same."

"Thank goodness. You do recall that it fell off in the shower yesterday?"

"I know," she said soothingly. "But it reattached readily enough. It'll be okay. May I show you?"

"Be gentle."

"I would, if you'd just slow down a little. Let me do it by myself!"

He complained, "You're too slow."

"Cut it out! I can do that!"

He told her, "We have to get back to the house before dark."

"Why?"

"I need to tell the guests goodbye."

She dismissed the need. "John and Margot are there."

He went completely still. His smile spread. He said, "Yeah." Then he settled his hips and wiggled them around a little, wiggling her, and he said, "Do your damnedest."

So she did.

The green condom didn't influence any part of the endeavor.

* * *

They went out and swam in the pond. There weren't any alligators in it as he'd mentioned. She looked. And she did swim, but she was cautious. However, the dog patrolled the perimeter and apparently didn't see anything remiss.

And Lemon dived in and didn't seem at all careful, so she became more assured.

She met him in the middle of the pond and told him, "Men are strange."

"Because they wear green condoms?"

"No, we've proven that is not a problem. Are other men like you?"

"I'm one of the lesser ones." He said that with modest earnestness. He did not believe any such thing.

She knew that. She said, "If you are any indication of it, men are only unusual. Their thinking is lopsided. They are mostly competitive. They plot and plan and blunder. And they're marvelous toys."

"We do tend to collect machinery. Possessions. Women."

"I didn't say you collected toys. I said you are toys. You are all toys."

He was indignant. "We run the whole shebang! What'd'ya mean *we*'re the toys?"

"We get to play with you."

"Welllll now, I do believe most men are willing to allow a female to play around with him."

"Allow? You didn't lure me out here for another skirmish?"

He was shocked at the very idea of such underhandedness. "No. I thought you might be interested in...the new grass and the solution to sludge. I thought that would entertain you.''

''I have never found sludge even interesting.''

In a more serious tone, he told her, ''You haven't been to the beaches that are closed because the ocean currents have brought the dumpings ashore.''

''That is true. There are TV specials on world trash dumps. In the middle of nowhere with the most beautiful or stark scenery, there are trash dumps. It is so shocking. Out in the desert, here, in this country. It is obscene.''

He responded in agreement, ''I do agree about the discard dumps. That's why I said everything needed the ability to rot. TV sets, old cars, toasters, magazines. The whole kaboodle. And besides all that, I wanted you to see how we handle shipping the cattle.''

''So this wasn't a way of escaping the house and having a little sex.''

''A little!'' He was shocked. ''You emptied me, all the way, so completely, look, I float.'' He lay back on the water and floated.

She laughed and tried her best to drown him. He did resist. But he didn't duck her. He was careful of her. He played and captured her and ran his hands over her naked body, under the water. He held her in outrageously personal ways, but he didn't duck her or threaten her or do anything roughly. He was naughty and wicked and sexual, but he was careful of her.

She was aware of that.

When they finally dragged their bodies out of the water and walked like Adam and Eve back to their scattered clothes, it turned out that he had food in his saddlebags. She said, "You planned to be out here this whole day."

He smiled. "I hadn't realized the food was there until I unsaddled the horse. The guys just automatically add food when they saddle up a horse. Food and a canteen of water. A guy never knows when a siren might lure an innocent man into a magical lagoon and have her wicked way with him. He needs sustenance."

She lay back with her shirt covering her body. Her long, bare legs and bare feet were modestly arranged in an attractive way. Her hair was drying and little curls were along her hairline. She was exquisite. She chewed another bite before she mentioned, "These huge sandwiches are different from those discreet ones served to the bridge people on Friday noon."

"Those lily-livered nothings?"

"I hadn't known lilies had livers."

He was shocked. "I would never in this world have guessed you were one of those kinds of people who played with words."

"I never do. I'm practical, prosaic. Incorruptible and—"

"Well, I'm not so sure about that there last labeling. I've done a very good job of corrupting you just in this weekend."

"Who will mention it in polite society? Who would believe you, if we are even seen together. I look pure. You look like a tomcat."

"While it is tempting, I won't tell the kids."

She said quickly, "I thought you wore a condom each time."

"Well, I did. But I want you to hang around here for a while so's we can decide if this is really as serious as I think it is." He watched her, and his face was very serious. His voice was lightened and gentle as he told her, "I don't believe I can let you go."

She saw how serious he was, because his sun wrinkles had smoothed and the lines were white.

She agreed. "I understand. I feel the same way. I shall stay with you. I really think it would be a good idea if I slept alone. We aren't giving us enough of a chance to see beyond how great it is to have sex together."

"We make love."

"I was trying to use words that would distance us from what is happening."

Eventually, they dressed in great leisure, and he watched her as he fumbled with his own clothing. He resaddled the patient horses and led them from the corral. The two riders mounted and looked around their Eden. He whistled for the dog. Then, with some regret, they returned to Lemon's great house.

It was dusk. Almost all the guests had departed. Theo had not. He came out of the house with John and Margot. But he wasn't blind and saw what was there between Lemon and that magical Renata. It was plain.

Theo made his goodbyes, and Lemon saw the anguish in Theo's relinquishing glances at what-might-have-been.

With the last of the guests gone, Lemon told the cook and the barn cat, Dan, "Thank you for filling in. You obviously played superbly. I'm proud of you." He shook their hands and was quite charming.

John watched those two going down the hall to the back of the house together, and he said offhandedly to Lemon, "CNN called, asking if you're going down the drain."

"Ted called?"

Margot replied, "Yes. He wants to know if you'd like to give your side."

"How nice of him. I can't believe this."

Margot explained, "They do it all the time on the business reports."

Lemon frowned. "Then, John, you do it. You go on camera and tell them the answers."

"Like what?"

"Oh, you know, we're solid. Wait for the semiannual CPA business reports. All is in a healthy financial condition. While if the stock is sold lower than the purchase price, it will readjust. Those are good buys. If anyone hears of the stock being sold, buy. It'll be profitable."

John said, "I know all that. But, Lemon, you ought to do it yourself."

Lemon was surprised. "It's good publicity. You'll get all kinds of offers, and I'll have to raise your meager pay."

John was patient, waiting.

Lemon was serious. Gesturing, he said, "You qualify. You're my financial adviser. You do it. Wear a navy—"

"Blue suit, a white shirt and a red tie." John interrupted. "I know, I know. Are you sure you don't want to handle this personally?"

Lemon smiled. "I'm an elusive, quirky man. I don't need the publicity. You're my front. Take Margot along. She can sit and worship you as you expound on this nonsense."

Yet again, John advised, "Remember. After this, when you're trying to avoid a pushy woman, choose another way."

And Lemon smiled. "I doubt the problem ever comes up for the rest of my life."

Margot said to John, "How can he be so dense? He'll never be free of women."

Lemon said, "We'll see." And he smiled at Renata.

Margot asked John, "Already?"

"It only took us one evening in the library."

Margot frowned. "It must be this house."

John considered. Then he suggested to Margot, "We could start inviting unsuitable couples here and test the premise."

Margot asked Lemon, "Are you sure you want a loose cannon like John to represent you?"

"You don't have a business degree. It has to be John."

John did go into town and the CNN crew showed up and filmed John in his navy blue suit, white shirt and his neatly trimmed beard.

John said all the right things. All that Lemon had suggested. And John added that holders of Lemon's stocks shouldn't panic. "Our examination of the unaudited financial reports in the last three months indicates all are in a healthy financial condition. Some have higher profits than others. In the long term, all will readjust. These are good buys."

The interview was on the financial section on the weekend, and John had to set up a phone line to take the calls at their offices. John mentioned that to Lemon and was somewhat disgruntled.

Lemon replied nicely, "I understand Margot is replying to the women who've written to you."

"Be quiet."

The days after that went so wonderfully. Renata never did convince Lemon they should sleep at night in their own beds. And their idyll was uninterrupted.

So the crew's holiday was over, and the men drifted back, eager to be back at work. That was a clue as to the kind of boss Lemon was. And Clint Terrell, the prairie wolf, came home.

Lemon greeted his foreman with a grin and handshake. "So you're back in one piece. How was it?"

Clint was a little somber. He groused, "I don't see how these things can happen to human people. I believe it's a matter of weapons. Those without can never win. They can't change their circumstances. Without guns to defend themselves, they're victims."

Lemon said to Clint, "Come sit down and tell me about it. This is Renata Gunther, who is my love."

As he sat down, Clint said, "Well, damn. He saw you first. That's mean. I'll probably never recover."

Lemon said, "Don't pay any attention to him. He's a prairie wolf. They're the worst kind."

Just then Hunter came quickly into the room to stop in the doorway where he stood and looked at Clint. He stared. Then he barked his low, serious bark once, very urgently.

Clint said, "Hey, boy, you don't bark thataway in the house. Hush, now."

And the dog went to Clint, whining low and almost desperately.

"You lost?"

The dog raised his head between Clint's hands and looked the big man in the face. He made no further sound.

Lemon said, "John's brother found the dog out along a road, over southeast of here. People tried to trap him, but no one ever did. He'd been around for some time. He's been looking for somebody."

"This looks like a dog my cousin had as a pup. Charlie was killed in a car crash about three years ago. We never found the dog. Do you suppose this could be Leo?"

With the saying of his name, the dog barked once and wagged his tail in whippings.

Tears formed in Clint's serious eyes. "Leo." It was almost a whisper. "My God. Leo. We got you back. Now if we could just find a way to get Charlie back."

And the dog barked once more.

"It *is* Leo!"

*   *   *   *   *

... *To be continued in Clint's story, Silhouette Desire's Man of the Month, December 1994,* An Obsolete Man.

MILLION DOLLAR SWEEPSTAKES (III)

No purchase necessary. To enter, follow the directions published. Method of entry may vary. For eligibility, entries must be received no later than March 31, 1996. No liability is assumed for printing errors, lost, late or misdirected entries. Odds of winning are determined by the number of eligible entries distributed and received. Prizewinners will be determined no later than June 30, 1996.

Sweepstakes open to residents of the U.S. (except Puerto Rico), Canada, Europe and Taiwan who are 18 years of age or older. All applicable laws and regulations apply. Sweepstakes offer void wherever prohibited by law. Values of all prizes are in U.S. currency. This sweepstakes is presented by Torstar Corp., its subsidiaries and affiliates, in conjunction with book, merchandise and/or product offerings. For a copy of the Official Rules send a self-addressed, stamped envelope (WA residents need not affix return postage) to: MILLION DOLLAR SWEEPSTAKES (III) Rules, P.O. Box 4573, Blair, NE 68009, USA.

EXTRA BONUS PRIZE DRAWING

No purchase necessary. The Extra Bonus Prize will be awarded in a random drawing to be conducted no later than 5/30/96 from among all entries received. To qualify, entries must be received by 3/31/96 and comply with published directions. Drawing open to residents of the U.S. (except Puerto Rico), Canada, Europe and Taiwan who are 18 years of age or older. All applicable laws and regulations apply; offer void wherever prohibited by law. Odds of winning are dependent upon number of eligibile entries received. Prize is valued in U.S. currency. The offer is presented by Torstar Corp., its subsidiaries and affiliates in conjunction with book, merchandise and/or product offering. For a copy of the Official Rules governing this sweepstakes, send a self-addressed, stamped envelope (WA residents need not affix return postage) to: Extra Bonus Prize Drawing Rules, P.O. Box 4590, Blair, NE 68009, USA.

SWP-S994

The Loop™

Is the future what it's cracked up to be?

This September, tune in to see why Jessica's partying days are over in

GETTING IT RIGHT: JESSICA
by Carla Cassidy

She had flunked out of college and nearly out of life. Her father expected her to come crawling home, and her friends expected her to fall off the wagon…but Jessica decided she'd rather sell her soul before she screwed up again. So she squeezed into an apartment with some girls she barely knew, got a job that barely paid the bills and decided that things were looking up. Trouble was, no one knew better than her that *looks* could be deceiving.

The ups and downs of modern life continue with

GETTING REAL: CHRISTOPHER
by Kathryn Jensen in October

GETTING PERSONAL: BECKY
by Janet Quin Harkin in November

Get smart. Get into "The Loop!"

Only from

Silhouette®

where passion lives.

LOOP2

Dark secrets, dangerous desire...

Lovers DARK AND DANGEROUS

Three spine-tingling tales from the dark side
of love.

This October, enter the world of shadowy
romance as Silhouette presents the third in their
annual tradition of thrilling love stories and
chilling story lines. Written by three of
Silhouette's top names:

LINDSAY McKENNA
LEE KARR
RACHEL LEE

Haunting a store near you this October.

Only from *Silhouette*®

...where passion lives.

This September, discover the fun of falling in love with...

Love and Laughter

Harlequin is pleased to bring you this exciting new collection of three original short stories by bestselling authors!

ELISE TITLE
BARBARA BRETTON
LASS SMALL

LOVE AND LAUGHTER—sexy, romantic, fun stories guaranteed to tickle your funny bone and fuel your fantasies!

Available in September wherever Harlequin books are sold.

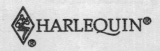

HARLEQUIN®

Coming in September from Joan Johnston

CHILDREN OF

Remember the Whitelaws of Texas from Joan Johnston's bestselling series *Hawk's Way?* Well, they settled down to have three sweet and innocent little kids. Now those little Whitelaws are all grown up—and not so innocent! And Silhouette Desire has captured their stories in a very sexy miniseries—*Children of Hawk's Way*.

Why is gorgeous rancher Falcon Whitelaw marrying a widowed mother who'd rather sleep with a rattlesnake than him?

Find out in Book One, *The Unforgiving Bride* (SD #878), coming your way this September...only from

Ginny / Donna / KEL

Also available by popular author

LASS SMALL

Silhouette Desire®

#05655	THE MOLLY Q	$2.75	☐
#05684	*'TWAS THE NIGHT	$2.79	☐
#05697	DOMINIC	$2.89	☐
#05830	A NEW YEAR	$2.99	☐
#05848	I'M GONNA GET YOU	$2.99	☐
	The following titles are part of the Fabulous Brown Brothers miniseries		
#05731	A RESTLESS MAN	$2.89	☐
#05755	BEWARE OF WIDOWS	$2.89	☐
#05800	BALANCED	$2.99	☐
#05817	*TWEED	$2.99	☐
#05860	SALTY AND FELICIA	$2.99 U.S.	☐
	*Man of the Month	$3.50 CAN.	
	(limited quantities available on certain titles)		

TOTAL AMOUNT	$	
POSTAGE & HANDLING	$	
($1.00 for one book, 50¢ for each additional)		
APPLICABLE TAXES**	$_____	
TOTAL PAYABLE	$_____	
(check or money order—please do not send cash)		

To order, complete this form and send it, along with a check or money order for the total above, payable to Silhouette Books, to: **In the U.S.:** 3010 Walden Avenue, P.O. Box 9077, Buffalo, NY 14269-9077; **In Canada:** P.O. Box 636, Fort Erie, Ontario, L2A 5X3.

Name:_____

Address:_____ City:_____

State/Prov.:_____ Zip/Postal Code:_____

**New York residents remit applicable sales taxes.
  Canadian residents remit applicable GST and provincial taxes.

SLSBACK3

♥ *Silhouette*®
TM